Dirk Prine never made a promise he didn't keep—even if it killed him.

★

Holtzer was sucking for air but Dirk could see no wound, no reason, until he pulled the bedroll away and saw Holtzer's stomach.

Knives.

His whole stomach was cut to pieces, bits of his guts sticking out through his hands. He was gurgling in pain, grunting with the effort of trying to push the guts back in.

Oh, God, Dirk thought. The bastards have killed him and he just won't die.

"Pr . . . Pr . . . Prine."

"Yes. I'm here," Dirk answered.

"Is . . . it . . . bad?"

Dirk hesitated. "Yes. It's bad. The worst."

"Damn. . . ."

Oh, yes, Dirk thought. Damn is right. Damn, damn, damn.

"Ta . . . take berries. Sell. Address in coat. Family. Send money. Please."

"I will," Dirk said, realizing that he meant it. Promised it. "I will."

Also by Paul Garrisen

DIRK'S RUN

Published by
HARPER PAPERBACKS

PAUL GARRISEN

DIRK'S REVENGE

Harper Paperbacks

Harper & Row, Publishers, New York
Grand Rapids, Philadelphia, St. Louis, San Francisco
London, Singapore, Sydney, Tokyo, Toronto

This is a work of fiction. The characters, incidents, and dialogues are products of the author's imagination and are not to be construed as real. Any resemblance to actual events or persons, living or dead, is entirely coincidental.

Harper Paperbacks a division of Harper & Row, Publishers, Inc.
10 East 53rd Street, New York, N.Y. 10022

Cover art by George Bush

First printing: May, 1990

Printed in the United States of America

10 9 8 7 6 5 4 3 2 1

DIRK'S REVENGE

CHAPTER 1

"I'M going to blow your ass through that back wall."

Dirk stopped with the mug of warm beer halfway up to his mouth and looked down the length of the bar, to the curve near the door, where an enormous hulk of a man held a Colt across the plank surface of the bar aimed at the center of Dirk's chest and thought, no.

No.

Up from Taos to Denver, off a horse and into a bar and order a beer just in time to have some drunk shoot him.

For no reason.

No.

"But. . . ." Dirk started. "But I don't even know you."

"The hell you don't. I'm Dan Bates and you shot my Eunice."

"I what?"

"You shot my Eunice, killed her dead." Bates wiped a tear from his eye. His body weaved but the gun—the goddamn gun, as Dirk thought of it—seemed to remain rock steady on about his third shirt button above his waist. It was not cocked but Bates's thumb was on the hammer. Maybe when/if he cocked it, the barrel would move off a little.

"I don't even know a Eunice. Never have." He had to get the big man talking, get the gun to move even a little, and he could try for his own. Try to get a shot off. Christ. It was stupid. He just wanted a beer and then he was going to head up into the diggings to see what that was like. Maybe stake a claim and get rich.

And now this.

No.

There had been eight or ten men at the bar and they pretty much evaporated back away from the line of fire. The bartender, who was bald and had an open shirt with a huge hairy belly sticking out, seemed to suck the stomach in a foot but he could not move any farther back. He watched Bates and every second or two slid his eyes to a couple of pegs beneath the bar where there was a stout hickory pick handle he used for settling arguments.

"Eunice," Bates said, "was the best goddamn coon hound a man ever had and you went and shot her for shitting on your boot and by God I'm going to kill you for it."

Bates cocked the Colt and as Dirk had hoped the sudden movement of his thumb jerked the barrel sideways enough to move it off Dirk. Dirk dropped as if his legs had collapsed—which they nearly had—and on the way down he pulled his own gun.

There were three shots over him, the third one dragging splinters off the bar, then a sound like somebody dropping meat. He took a deep breath, let it out, and stood and fired four times as fast as he could.

At nothing.

As near as Dirk could figure all four shots went somewhere in the general vicinity of the man he'd been trying to hit. But there wasn't time to aim, time to do anything but shoot.

The huge man was gone. Everything had happened so fast that for a second Dirk thought he'd hit him with his first shot and dropped him behind the bar.

Then he realized what he was seeing. Everybody in the bar had either gone out the door or dropped on the first shot.

Everybody that is but the bartender. He was

holding the hickory pick handle and was mashed flat back against the back bar, his eyes squinched shut.

It all registered on Dirk's brain. The bartender had used the pick handle to drop Bates—that had been the meaty sound.

Then Dirk had stood and fired without thinking.

There were four bullet holes spread across a good four feet of the front window.

None of them, somehow, had hit the bartender. Considering the spread of Dirk's shots that wasn't too surprising.

I could run a horse through that group, he thought.

"Jesus," the bartender said, blowing the cloud of smoke from his face. "You like to made me shit my pants. . . ."

For all of that he didn't seem too rattled. He looked over the bar at the man he'd hit and grunted. "I hit him a touch harder than I meant to—he'll be sore when he comes around."

"I'm sorry about all this," Dirk said. "I didn't know you'd dropped him."

"Wouldn't have mattered." The bartender shrugged. "You wouldn't have hit him anyway. You want a beer while we talk about how you're going to pay for the window?"

"Pay?" Dirk reloaded while he spoke. Old army habits die hard. He'd cleaned his musket one night and not reloaded, thinking there'd be drier powder available the next morning. That night they'd been hit by Reb cavalry and he had naught but his bayonet. He still thought about the bayonet sometimes—three, no, four years later. He'd pushed it into a Reb's stomach just above the belt buckle and the Reb looked at him as if to apologize for running onto the bayonet. It made for a bad thought. "I didn't start this ball rolling."

"No. But you didn't have to shoot and you did, and you shot so poorly you took my window out. Cost me a hundred and sixty dollars, freight included from St. Louis."

Might as well be a thousand, Dirk thought. He had about six dollars to his name—and his horse and saddle. Enough for a good meal and to leave Denver. Just. Anything more was out of the question. "I don't have it."

"We have law here." The bartender smiled. "Way it works they arrest you, then you work at fifty cents a day until I get my money. The work is interesting—cleaning outhouses and horse shit off the streets. It builds character."

Or I could ride, Dirk thought. Just jog on the hell out of here. He studied the distance to the door. Customers had drifted back in and partially blocked the way, but he still thought he could beat the bartender.

"Perhaps that won't be necessary."

Dirk turned to the voice and for the first time noticed a man sitting back in the corner of the saloon at a rough wood table. He was dressed in a dark suit.

"I'm Derek Holtzer. And I might be able to help you pay for the window."

"I'm Duncan Prine, but people call me Dirk."

Dirk found himself facing the man. The man's suit was dusty on the shoulders but buttoned tightly so the man stood straight. He looked, Dirk thought, like a stovepipe—a forty-year-old, bald stovepipe. He was holding a mug of beer, half finished, and he gestured to a table back in the corner.

"Would you like a beer?"

Dirk hesitated. Men had come back into the bar and were bellying up for drinks. But the man on the floor was still out—others were stepping over him to get beer—and he might be mean when he came out of it. *If* he came out of it. That pick handle sounded like it went through the skull bone. He might die there, or come around and spend the rest of his life drooling. Dirk had seen it before in bar fights.

Dirk nodded. "Sure." He followed the older man to the corner table. The bartender brought a pitcher and walked back to the bar.

"Thank you," Dirk said, "for the beer and saying that about the window. But I don't need the help. . . ."

"It doesn't look that way to me." He took a sip of his beer, swallowed—his Adam's apple fighting to slide past the tight collar. "He seems to have you locked up pretty tight. Either you pay for the window or you go to jail. . . ."

Dirk shrugged. "It will cool down. I'll just wait and slide away later. . . ."

"I don't think so. The bartender is taking your horse right now."

"What . . . ?"

Dirk turned and saw through the broken window that Holtzer was right. The bartender had untied his bay and was letting another man lead it away. He rose but Holtzer reached across the table and stopped him.

"Believe me," Holtzer said. "You can't win in this game. I've been here two weeks and seen the bartender work. He really knows the law here and if you don't pay for the window you're going to jail."

"But that's my *horse*!" Dirk stared. "Hell, man, they can't take a man's *horse*. Up north—in Wyoming—they'd hang him for that."

Holtzer nodded. "But he knows the constable here."

"Damn. . . ."

Holtzer waited a moment, took another swallow of beer, then cleared his throat.

"I liked the way you handled that situation," he said.

"You did?" Dirk settled back into the chair and drank some beer. "I seem to remember spending most of my time on my ass hiding in back of the bar."

"You shot back."

"And missed everything I shot at." Dirk smiled ruefully. "I'm damn lucky I didn't hit my own horse."

"Still. You reacted well in the face of adversity."

Dirk studied Holtzer. He spoke so strangely—his words coming out almost as stiff as the suit looked. Not from the West, Dirk thought—definitely not from the West. But the accent didn't seem eastern, either. Dirk was from Pennsylvania—years back by way of the war and a Reb ball and a lot of riding—and Holtzer's accent wasn't from the East. "If you mean I didn't shit my pants you're right. Just."

Holtzer smiled. "Most men would have done just that. The point is, I have need of your services. I will pay for the window and give you two hundred dollars besides—all for two weeks' work. Perhaps less."

Dirk finished his beer and stood up. "Well, I'd better be going. . . ."

"What's the matter?" Holtzer held up his hand. "Why are you leaving?"

"Nobody pays that kind of money for work

unless it's illegal and I've already got enough trouble with the law."

"Let me assure you, Mr. Prine, there is nothing whatever illegal in what I propose."

Dirk turned. Something in Holtzer's voice stopped him. "What do you want me to do?"

Holtzer hesitated. He poured more beer in Dirk's mug. "I want you to guard me and a cargo I plan to freight up to Central City." He pointed to the back of the saloon, which was west. "That's a mining town up in the mountains west of Denver."

"I've heard of it." Dirk nodded. The town was a rough mining boom town, full of miners and whores. A wild place. All the stories Dirk had heard about it ended in somebody getting shot all to hell. "You said guard—what do I have to guard?"

Holtzer cleared his throat.

"Strawberries."

Dirk stared at him. "What?"

"I said 'strawberries'—I want you to guard a load of strawberries that I'm going to haul up to Central City."

CHAPTER

☆ 2 ☆

DIRK swore as the wagon wheel caught a sharp rock. The sharpness of the rock came through the steel wagon tire, through the hardwood spokes, and seemed to focus directly into his spine. It did not help that he had gotten cross-eyed on needle beer the night before, trying to drink Holtzer under the table. Trying and failing. His head felt like it was going to explode any moment—just splatter into the morning sun—and his mouth tasted like he'd been sucking on a barn for a week.

"Beautiful morning, isn't it?"

Holtzer sat next to him on the wagon seat. He looked fresh, clean, clear-eyed, and was still, incredibly, wearing a suit and a tie with a cellulose collar. He had a wide smile on his face and he slapped Dirk on the shoulder, causing him to wince as his head jerked.

Dirk was driving the team and when the wagon hit the rock they all but stopped. They were, up and down, the worst horses he had ever seen. Old, their backbones jutted up like furry fingers, and Dirk could have played a tune on their ribs. He couldn't possibly see how the team could pull the wagon up the winding canyons into the mountains to Central City. Forty miles or more, and the wagon. . . .

The wagon was a brand-new freighter with high wooden sides, painted a bright green with red pinstripes around the sides. The wheels were still tight—the spokes hadn't loosened and began creaking.

That morning he had helped load the wagon.

Strawberries—Holtzer had not been lying. They took the team out of the livery and drove the wagon to the icehouse on the ramshackle edge of Denver. Blocks of ice were brought down from lakes in the winter and stored in sawdust. Holtzer covered the bottom of the wagon with ice—supervising Dirk and two men from the icehouse but not doing the work himself. When it was completely covered, a foot thick, he directed Dirk to drive the team a mile to the railhead where they unloaded ten-pound boxes of strawberries from an iced railcar.

There were eighty boxes and Dirk carried each one himself, packing them carefully down on the icy bed in the wagon. When they were loaded Holtzer had Dirk shovel sawdust from the railcar on top of them until the wagon looked to be hauling a load of sawdust.

All of this before hard dawn. Eight hundred pounds of strawberries and they started on their way in the new sun.

Dirk slapped the reins across the rumps of the horses and spit off to the side. The work with the berries had sweated some of the beer out but he still felt like puking.

"Strawberries," he said out loud. It was almost swearing.

"What?" Holtzer had been looking ahead at the peaks. Though it was mid-July the mountains were still white-capped halfway down.

"I said 'strawberries,'" Dirk repeated. "I never thought I'd be guarding eight hundred pounds of strawberries."

"It's all business," Holtzer said. "A simple business speculation. I bought the berries for thirty cents a pound and I hope to sell them for a profit in Central City."

Dirk took a deep breath, let it out. His head throbbed but seemed to be settling down and he only felt like puking about half the time. "What kind of profit are you figuring on?"

Holtzer shrugged. "It's up in the air—I should

think the berries will bring about five dollars a pound. . . ."

"Four thousand dollars for strawberries?"

"Supply and demand." Holtzer shrugged. "It's simply a matter of supply and demand. Those miners have gold and no berries—I have berries and no gold. A simple exchange."

Dirk looked at the mountains, thinking. "That's close to ten years' wages for a man. For one load of berries."

"Business," Holtzer said again, as if it explained everything.

They rode in silence for the rest of the morning and into the afternoon. Holtzer sitting straight and Dirk sweating the rest of the beer away.

They worked into the foothills near the small town of Golden—itself a wild place. And as they moved into the foothills near Golden they suddenly entered what amounted to a stream of human flesh moving up into the mountains. Miners heading into the mountains—men, boys, even a few women made a continuous flowing highway of people. It was so sudden, so startling, that Dirk let off whipping the team. Bad as they were they stopped at once; blowing and sweating, stamping at the flies.

"Jesus," Dirk said, "look at them. . . ."

Holtzer was silent.

"There are hundreds of them."

"Thousands, I should think," Holtzer said. "All heading up after gold."

Dirk shook his head. "It's crazy. . . ."

They reminded him of ants somehow. It wasn't that they scurried. In fact most of them were almost invisible under loads. With knapsacks and crude wooden pack frames, some pulling wooden travois skids with pans and shovels for cargo. They trudged slowly in a long line past the wagon and up into the mountains.

Dirk could not see either end. To the right they came from Denver and to the left they disappeared up into the mountains, a living path.

"I've heard of this," Dirk said. "I mean you hear stories but I had no idea. . . ."

"Hey!" A man with a carved wooden pack frame stopped and called to them. "I'll pay you a hundred dollars if you'll carry this pack up to Central City for me."

But Holtzer shook his head and the man walked on, never really expecting help.

"What are we going to do?" Dirk asked.

"What do you mean?"

Dirk pointed up the trail. "They're all on foot. The wagon is so big. We'll run over them."

Before Holtzer could say anything a wagon appeared on the trail. It was small, a mud wagon altered with plank sides, and being pulled by one enormous old workhorse. It was piled high with bundles and packs. On the side of the wagon in black paint was lettered:

PLUNKETT FREIGHT CO. LTD.
FREIGHT FROM DENVER TO THE CLAIMS
WILLARD J. PLUNKETT, PROP.

Willard Plunkett—Dirk assumed that was the driver of the mud wagon—looked almost exactly like a gopher. He was squat, covered with dust and grime, and had a round face—so fat his cheeks looked stuffed with food. It proved to be tobacco juice. As he passed Dirk and Holtzer he spat a stream that looked to contain close to a quart of brown juice and nodded without speaking.

Dirk used the reins to pop the team into movement and they pulled in the line to the rear of the mud wagon and moved along.

"They're so quiet," Holtzer said. "So sad and quiet. . . ."

Dirk agreed but said nothing. Hanging off the sides of the seat was a linen water bag and for probably the tenth time he took a drink, swallowed deeply, and poured some over his head.

The afternoon heat worked down on them. Dirk was afraid to stop the team until they wanted to rest for the night. The team was so weak he wasn't sure he could get them going again. Three times he left Holtzer to drive the team and ran up alongside them with a canvas bucket to water them while working so they wouldn't get a chance to stop, and twice he had to tell people to get off the back of the wagon when they tried to sneak rides.

Slow as they went they made some progress and by dusk they were high in the foothills. A small mountain went up to their left, climbed into the gathering darkness.

"We'll have to stop for the night soon," Dirk said. "The team needs to rest." More like die, he thought but did not say—they need to die.

Holtzer nodded. "There's a wide place up ahead. Pull in there."

It was more than a wide part in the track. A trail went off to the left, wound back into a small side canyon, and Dirk pulled the team into it.

The horses were only too glad to stop and Dirk had trouble getting them to work hard enough to back the wagon around and aimed back toward the main track to leave in the morning.

They were in a wide, sandy area that was—strangely—without people. Farther up the small canyon Dirk could see people setting up tarp lean-tos and below he could see the seemingly endless stream of people heading up to the claims in the mountains.

But here they were alone. Dirk unharnessed and watered the team, gave each of them half a pound of oats, then pulled his bedroll from the wagon. He hobbled them and tied them to a long rope. There were some small tufts of green grass near the stream for them to graze on but it was bad grass—water grass was weak grass—and he knew he would have to give them more oats in the morning before starting. They might not have enough oats. There might not be enough oats in the whole world for these horses.

Holtzer watched him but stood by the wagon.

Dirk stopped. "We're going to lay up for the night—rest the team. Make camp."

Holtzer nodded. "I understand. It's just that I never . . . camped."

"What?"

"I've never made a camp."

Dirk stared at him, the bedroll hanging in his hand. "But you came west, you're here."

"I came from Europe on a ship, and then by train to Denver. In Europe I was born and lived in a large city—Geneva, Switzerland. I have never slept out on the ground."

Dirk almost couldn't believe him. In the four and a half years since leaving the army and traveling, he had spent so many nights on the ground that he felt strange in a room. And here was a man who had *never* slept outside?

"Do you have a bedroll?"

"I have a blanket and tarp a man in a store

in Denver sold me. I would assume that I use them somehow."

Dirk nodded. "Get them out of the wagon and I'll show you how to get set up. Then we'll eat. . . ."

Holtzer turned and dragged down his tarp and blanket and they settled in for the night.

CHAPTER 3

IT proved to be a miserable camp and a miserable night. Try as they might they couldn't find a single stick of firewood. The thousands of miners had long before used up even the smallest twigs. Dirk could not find even dry grass or brush. The land was stripped of anything burnable.

So they made a cold camp. There was a stream in the bed of the creek near the track. They had water.

But without fire they couldn't cook beans or coffee or bacon. Luckily Holtzer had bought two loaves of sourdough bread and a sack of hard candy along with the flour and beans and bacon. For the night meal they had bread and cold water with a piece of hard candy to suck on for dessert.

Dirk showed Holtzer how to make a bed and the two of them crawled in to sleep not long after dark.

Just before lying back Dirk took his Colt out of the holster and lay it near his head. He felt silly doing it—it was such a greenhorn thing to do. As a matter of fact he had actually read a passage in a dime novel about a cowboy named Billy who "...slept with his gun for a pillow," and laughed when he read it. But in this case he had a reason for it.

The trail was filled with greedy, desperate men. The men who went to the claims, Dirk knew, were often the lowest men on earth. They were men and women nobody else wanted—most of them would find nothing in the mountains. Hard scrabble men who would kill Holtzer and Dirk for the clothes they wore—let alone four thousand dollars' worth of berries.

Having the Colt ready just made sense.

And besides, Dirk saw Holtzer nod with approval. Whatever else, he was the boss and paying good money for Dirk. If he approved of Dirk using his gun for a pillow, so be it.

So he lay the Colt next to his head, the hammer down on an empty chamber, and fell into a light sleep.

The light sleep and the ready Colt were the only things that saved his life.

Sadly, they did not do the same for Holtzer.

He dreamt of the war.

It was the same dream he'd had a hundred and more times since the end of the war.

It was a dream of getting hit.

He'd had a friend named Peter Harkness. Peter had been next to him in back of a fence and the Rebs were pouring it to them, firing so fast in volleys their fire sounded like a giant ripping cloth. A great tearing sound.

Peter turned to him and smiled and was about to say something to Dirk—some important thing, some small thing, some new thing, some old thing—Dirk would never know.

A Reb minié ball took Peter in the temple—went in one temple and out the other in an almost perfect line and carried away all the things Peter would ever say again in a splattering cloud of brain.

But. . . .

Dirk thought just that. But. . . . But what was he going to say? What was Peter going to say?

That much of the dream was true. Dirk had a friend named Peter who had died in just such a way.

Then the Rebs had charged, and carried the line and overrun their position and a Reb officer had aimed at him and smiled and put a ball in him. In his leg.

That much was also true.

But in the dream it changed. In the dream the Reb officer just looked at him and smiled and his arm had moved sideways and he didn't shoot and instead Dirk looked down at his leg and aimed his own gun down at his thigh and pulled the trigger only the gun didn't go off.

He tried and tried and it wouldn't fire and then his eyes snapped open and he was awake.

In almost pitch-darkness.

There was no moon and clouds hid most of the stars and he lay sweating in his bedroll for a few seconds, thinking of the dream, when he heard the sound.

It was a scrape of metal on metal.

No sound in nature was like it. No night birds or movement of wind or the water sounds was like it. Metal scraping on metal. At the wagon.

He grabbed the Colt and sat up, his thumb on the hammer, starting to call out.

Then he saw shapes.

Two, three men—the shapes blurred together and were hard to decipher—were by the wagon.

Another sound stopped him. It was a gurgling, wet-spit sound.

Coming from Holtzer's bedroll.

All of this in seconds. And in the same time

he sensed-felt-saw another form, another man, leaning over him from the side.

He fired. Straight up and to the right, up into the man, and in the flash of the gunpowder—as bright as lightning—he saw that his bullet had taken the man square in the chest. It picked him up, threw him back, and before the gun-flash light was gone Dirk turned to the others and fired again. Three more times, as fast as he could.

Save one.

Save one bullet if the bastards came in on him. Save one to take one more of them down.

But in the three flashes he saw them run. He thought he might have hit one—somebody swore and screamed—but they all moved well enough and in seconds even the sound of their footsteps had gone down the trail and Dirk was left in silence broken only by the sound of gurgling coming from Holtzer's bedroll.

He exhaled and took a deep breath, realized he had held it all the while he was shooting. Then he reloaded, popping the loading gate out with his thumb and pulling cartridges from his belt in the darkness, dropping them in.

He wanted to get to Holtzer but there was still the other man. He'd been hit but hit men were not always safe men. He cocked the Colt again, stepped to the downed man, and thumbed a match, the Colt ready. But he needn't have worried. The bullet had taken his heart and he was gone.

Then to Holtzer.

He struck another match and kneeled. Holtzer was sucking for air but Dirk could see no wound, no reason, until he pulled the bedroll away and saw his stomach.

They had used a knife on the sleeping man. They must have come on him as they went toward the wagon and they used a knife on him.

Knives.

His whole stomach was cut to pieces, bits of his guts sticking out through his hands. He was gurgling in pain, grunting with the effort of trying to push the guts back in.

Oh, Dirk thought—oh, God. The bastards have killed him and he just won't die.

"Pr . . . Pr . . . Prine."

Holtzer worked to get it out.

"Yes. I'm here," Dirk answered.

"Is . . . it . . . bad?"

Dirk hesitated. What the hell, no sense lying to him. The match burned out and he did not strike another. He didn't need to see more. Holtzer would die—soon or a bit later. Dirk hoped soon, knowing how painful gut wounds were. "Yes. It's bad. The worst."

"Damn. . . ."

Oh, yes, Dirk thought. Damn is right. Damn, damn, damn.

"Ta . . . take berries. Sell. Address in coat. Family. Send money. Please."

Dirk nodded, forgetting Holtzer could not see him in the darkness.

"Please!" Holtzer repeated, thinking Dirk was refusing him.

"I will," Dirk said, realizing that he meant it. Promised it. "I will."

"Go . . . good."

After that he was silent for a while and Dirk kneeled there, holding his head, waiting, and still later he said some things in a foreign language that sounded like German. Then there was nothing for a time, only the gurgling, and when that stopped and Dirk could feel that he wasn't breathing any longer he struck another match and saw that he was dead. Dirk settled Holtzer's head back down gently and thought how far it was from the mountains of Colorado to Geneva, Switzerland.

Damn.

CHAPTER 4

IN the half-light of dawn he dragged the body of the man he had killed to a point between two rocks and jammed it in, mostly out of sight. He did not feel he owed the man more.

But Holtzer was a different matter. There was a shovel in the wagon—along with an axe, a pick, food enough for two men for a month, and a new Colt and black holster that Holtzer hadn't worn. The owner of the store must have seen him coming, Dirk thought, looking at the gear and food. The Colt had probably never been loaded.

As soon as there was light—and he cursed himself for not thinking to tell Holtzer to get a lantern and some oil—he found a flat spot up above the creek where there was a small view and he dug a four-foot-deep grave. He would have gone deeper but he hit hard pan at that level and it was impossible to dig more.

He had nothing to write with so he used his pocket knife to carve Holtzer's name on a piece of wood he broke from the wagon. It wouldn't last. Some miner would burn it to heat coffee, probably, but he felt he had to do something, leave something of the man.

He wrapped the body in the bedroll—in truth Holtzer had never left it—and carried it to the grave. It took some horsing—Holtzer was heavier than he first seemed—but he finally positioned the body in the bottom and climbed out. The bedroll had come away from Holtzer's face and he leaned down to pull it back over before shoveling dirt and while he was leaning he heard the voice in back of him.

"Died of the flux, did he?"

It was a raspy voice and took Dirk completely by surprise. His nerves were raw anyway and almost without thinking he rolled sideways onto his back and jerked his Colt. It was not a smooth movement and he all but dropped the gun and in any event had it out way too late to do any good had it been a real threat.

He found himself looking up at a thin, tall man—who looked somewhat like a more fully bearded Lincoln—and a strange-looking boy in a floppy hat and loosely fitting clothes that hung in folds. The boy had huge brown eyes, deer eyes, almost hidden by the hat. They were wearing packs and it was astonishing to Dirk that they could have walked up on him while he was digging without his hearing them, until he saw they were wearing worn legging moccasins.

"It would be better if you didn't shoot us. Sam and me mean you no harm." The man stood quietly, simply. He did not seem to be armed and the boy had no weapon either.

Still on his back, Dirk put the gun away. "Sorry. I've had a rough night. He didn't die of the flux. Some dirt come on us during the night and cut his guts out."

The man leaned down and helped Dirk to his feet. The boy hung back, looking at the ground. He seemed to be very shy.

"I'm Ben McWilliams. And this is Sam. We were on our way to the diggings up at Central City and saw your wagon and thought we might catch a ride. I'm getting on and have a touch of ague now and again that makes me walk slow. We'd be glad to work it off somehow."

Dirk thought about it. He wouldn't mind the company and if there were many more incidents like last night it wouldn't hurt to have extra ears and eyes. "Can you shoot?"

Ben shook his head. "Unfortunately no. I am more inclined to speaking than violence—although I understand the need for it now and then. I believe it says in the Book that one must take an eye for an eye. . . ."

"Are you a minister?" Dirk hated the stumpers and wasn't about to have one with him on the wagon.

"Oh, no. Not by any stretch. I've done some reading of the law, some buying and selling of cattle and land but never the gospel." He gestured to the boy. "But even if I can't shoot, Sam here is a fair hand with a gun."

"He's not wearing one."

Ben coughed. "We arrived in Denver with very little. I had a small gun which we hoped to use for trail exigencies but it went for three pounds of potatoes and some flour. I'm afraid that was two and a half days ago and now we are out of food as well."

Well hell, Dirk thought. Why not. "Help me finish here and we'll get moving."

He stood for a moment, trying to think of something to say over Holtzer and there was nothing. He didn't know anything about the man, didn't know him at all. He turned to Ben. "You know anything to say at a burying?"

Ben shook his head. "Nothing religious. Just that we all return to dust and I hope he rests in peace, whoever he was."

"Holtzer. Mr. Holtzer."

"Amen." This came from Sam and Dirk

looked at the boy sharply. His voice was high, hadn't changed yet, except that he looked old enough for his nuts to have dropped.

"Yeah. Amen." Dirk had taken his hat off and he put it back on and picked up the shovel.

He started to fill the grave but Ben reached out before he hit the second shovelful.

"Let me. You can get the wagon ready. . . ."

Dirk nodded and went to the horses. They looked worse than they had the day before but Dirk knew appearances could be deceiving. If they lived and kept eating they would get better with each day—look worse for three or four days but be getting stronger with each mile. If they lived.

They were stiff and muscle-sore and shook their heads when he bridled them and put the harnesses on them. He backed them to the wagon and hooked them up, threw the reins up on the wagon seat.

"Pa," the boy's voice piped. "There's another body over here in these rocks."

Dirk looked up from the trace chain he was hooking to the singletree. Ben had paused at the grave and had a question in his eyes.

"That was one of the men who attacked us. I shot him."

"Shouldn't we bury him?"

"No." Dirk's voice was flat. "We shouldn't. Let the coyotes have him."

Still Ben waited. "But he's a man, isn't he?"

"He's scum. It doesn't matter if we bury him."

"But still. . . ."

Dirk stood from the trace chain and wiped sweat from his forehead. The sun was barely up and it was already hot. The war came to him. It was never far from him. There were men who came around for the bodies after a battle. Came in wagons and picked the bodies up like meat, like dead meat. They took them to pits. And in the aid stations, in the tents and farmhouses where they worked on the wounded they stacked the cut-off legs and arms in piles in back and the same men who took the bodies came with the wagons and took the limbs with the bodies to the pits and dumped them in piles. Then they took a team with a scraper and pulled dirt over the meat.

The dead meat.

He remembered the horses on the scraper and how they walked on the bodies and parts of bodies to pull the dirt over them. The drivers wore cloth over their mouths and they had pulled masks over the horses' mouths as well, tucking them under the bridles so they wouldn't have to breathe the smell of rotting meat.

And here this man worried about the body of one piece of trash.

Dirk shook his head, sighed. "I don't care. If you want to dig a grave go ahead. But I won't turn a hand for him."

Ben nodded. "I'll make it a shallow grave."

True to his word as soon as he finished filling Holtzer's grave he dug a small trench. The boy reluctantly helped him drag the body to it and they covered it with not more than a foot of dirt. Dirk knew the coyotes would dig him up anyway—as they might also dig Holtzer up. Coyotes were resourceful and always seemed to win.

"I'd like to get moving," Dirk said as soon as they were done. He tied his bay to the back of the wagon and swung up into the seat.

Ben put his and the boy's bundle on the back of the wagon and pulled himself up on the other side and the boy sat between them and Dirk popped the reins across the horses to get them moving. He had to hit them hard and swear—early in his life teamsters had convinced him of the need to swear when driving a team—before they jerked the load into movement. Once it was broken loose they pulled it more easily and Dirk let them make their own way back down to the main track.

Men were already making their way into the mountains.

Dirk waited. Ben still had not asked what was under the tarp in the wagon and Dirk had seen him look at it with curiosity. While he waited—because the team was so slow and they had so much time—Dirk studied the boy.

Something was wrong about him.

It wasn't necessarily a bad wrong, Dirk decided, just that he didn't seem quite right. He hadn't said much or done much but he moved funny—didn't move like a boy ought to move.

Too smooth. Too soft.

Jesus, Dirk thought, maybe he's a sweet Nancy. He'd met one in the army. One of the medical orderlies who'd worked on the wounded was a sweet Nancy and while nobody had ever seen him try anything everybody kept moving around him.

The boy's leg had been touching Dirk's as they rode and Dirk pulled his leg away quickly. He didn't want anything to do with sweet Nancys. . . .

"What's in the wagon?"

Ben finally asked and Dirk shook his head. He'd been watching Sam out of the corner of his eye, waiting for some overt sign or attempt before he threw both of them off the wagon and the question caught him off guard.

"Strawberries," he said, answering without thinking. "Eight hundred pounds of strawberries."

"Ahh." Ben nodded slowly. He didn't seem

surprised. "You intend selling them for a profit to the miners in Central City."

"He did. The dead man. I was just hired on to guard the berries. And him. I'm not much of a guard. . . ."

"These things happen."

Sam's leg came over against Dirk's again, pressing, and that was enough.

"All right—both of you, off the wagon." Dirk stopped the team. "Before I throw you off."

"What's the matter?" Ben turned from looking at the load, trying to see under the tarp.

"This whole business. I'm not sitting here with a sweet Nancy making cornflower eyes at me. You both hit the dirt or by God. . . ."

Ben turned to the boy. "Sam. Did you touch him?"

Sam said nothing.

"Answer me."

"Just on the leg. I just legged him a little, is all. Dammit, Pa, I can't help how I feel. It's warm and I got to thinking it would be nice to leg him a little."

"I'm sorry," Ben said to Dirk. "Sam is just coming into heavy puberty and it's enough to make a father go crazy. Honest to God, I sometimes don't know what's come over her. . . ."

"Her?" Dirk looked at Sam.

"Sam, take off your hat and show him."

Sam pulled the hat off and long chestnut curls

dropped down to frame her face. She turned her eyes up to Dirk and smiled and became in half an instant an exceptionally beautiful young woman.

CHAPTER 5

"SHE'S just nineteen," Ben said. "Her mother passed away when she was a sprite so she's never had the teachings of a woman and I think I have failed her. Sometimes I just don't understand her."

"Didn't you like it when I legged you?" Sam looked up at Dirk. The corners of her eyes tipped up slightly and the lids looked sleepy. Like a cat with a mouse, he thought.

"But Sam?" Dirk asked. "Why that name?"

"It's short for Samantha. When we decided to come to the diggings we thought it would be best for people to think she was a boy. You know, for protection."

Yes, Dirk thought, but to protect who? The

eyes were brown with flecks of some kind of green in them that caught the light and made him think of things he hadn't thought of in some time. A woman he'd known in Kansas. Margaret. With eyes like that. She was the daughter of a man he did some work for and they'd met in the moonlight and he thought of her now. An ache, the thought, a small pain of memory. He'd wanted to marry and she smiled and laughed him away but the same eyes. Up at the corners.

He shook his head.

"Well—maybe it would be better if she rode over on the side and you took the middle."

Sam shook her head in short anger, the hair whipping. "I never did nothing but leg him. . . ."

But she moved and Ben took the middle and they continued for a short time in silence. Sam had tucked the hair back under her hat but not before several men in the line of marchers had seen it and Dirk thought, Oh, good, now we've got that to deal with as well. The first time we stop for the night they'll come looking for her. To get legged.

Life, he thought, does it to me. Does what it wants to me. One day a man wants to kill me because I shot his coon hound and to keep from going to jail I wind up freighting a load of somebody else's berries so I can send the money to some other person I've never met after he gets killed and I wind up sitting next to a girl—woman, young woman—who likes to leg me.

Life.

He leaned back in the seat and let the sun loosen him up. He felt stiff from the night and digging the grave; body stiff and mind stiff. Two men dead and for what?

Berries.

Jesus, what a waste.

And maybe a third. He thought he had heard a bullet catch meat when he fired. A third man might be dead or dying.

Or would die when and if he caught them. He knew that. It couldn't be allowed. Not gutting a man like that while he slept and then just moving on. Chances are they would vanish—were just trail trash that would move on and vanish in the diggings and he would never see them again.

But if he did, and recognized them, it would have to be done. They'd have to be braced and put down.

All for berries.

The trail started to climb. Not steeply but enough so that the weight settled back on the team and slowed them. They were coming into a narrow canyon and the road was cut into the side of a cliff face. It was about twenty feet down to a roaring white-water river and no extra width for the wagon.

Dirk hoped that he didn't meet another wagon. There were dozens of men walking ahead and behind them, and barely enough room for that. If they met a wagon somebody would have to back up. And he didn't see how it was possible to back the horses and wagon down the canyon.

The sound of the river was so loud it made conversation difficult but Ben tried anyway.

"Do you have somebody ready to buy the berries when you get there?" He had to yell to overpower the sound of the river.

Dirk shook his head.

"There is some risk to the business endeavor then," Ben yelled. He nodded to himself, thinking. "You would do better if you had somebody to go ahead and get the situation ready. Otherwise you may get there and not be able to move all the berries before they spoil."

Dirk waited.

"I of course could do that for you. I could take your horse and ride ahead and spread the word and insure that there would be a market for your berries waiting when you arrived."

Dirk said nothing. His first inclination was to turn the deal down. He liked the bay a great deal, and had gone through a lot with the horse. Sending it off with a stranger was difficult to contemplate. Still, there was something to what Ben said. The ice wouldn't last for more than another day or perhaps two. Then the heat would start on the wagon and that would be it. In a matter of hours the berries would turn to mush.

"I naturally would want some small amount for the negotiations," Ben yelled. "But that can be worked out later. Just enough for a small stake."

Still Dirk waited, considering.

Ben mistook the waiting for doubt of his honesty. "If there is any doubt about my veracity, of course Sam would be with you."

Oh, Dirk thought, wonderful. That would make up for it. About like leaving a fox with the chickens.

And yet there was much truth in what Ben was saying. From what men had said who were walking the trail it was apparently not more than another day to Central City, maybe a day and a half. If Ben went on ahead he could put up a flier on a wall and it would help to move them fast. And riding Dirk's bay he would get there at least a day before they could get there in the wagon.

On the other hand there was Sam. How would he handle that? With just the two of them on the wagon seat and nobody between them it might prove ticklish.

He smiled at that. Ticklish. That was a good word for it.

Well, he'd have to take care of that when it happened.

Business was business.

God, he thought, listen to me. A busted-out saddle bum talking about business. Next I'll have a frock coat and a diamond stickpin and hire people to scratch me.

Against his better judgment he finally nodded.

CHAPTER

CENTRAL City was not something Dirk could believe.

As far back as the war he'd heard stories about the diggings out in California, how crazy they were, and so he was half prepared and still they were not believable.

The ride up had been strange enough.

Ben had gone on ahead on the bay. Dirk had watched him ride off through the walking men, the bay threading his way carefully, with some definite misgivings. Seeing somebody ride off on your horse was bad enough, but as soon as he was out of sight Sam slid over on the seat next to him and jammed her leg into his.

"We're alone," she said pointedly. "Just you and me on this seat."

The fact that they were not truly alone, were indeed surrounded by trekking miners and trail riffraff, didn't seem to bother her at all. She reached up and stuck her tongue in his ear, jamming it halfway through his head and making him jump sideways nearly off the wagon.

"Now wait a minute," he said, wiping the spit out of his ear. "You just take it easy. I'm not going to take advantage of you." Oh, yes, he thought, me take advantage of her? Right. "Your father left you in my keeping. It wouldn't be right."

"Oh, pig shit. How come you're so stuffy? Pa has left me lots of times with men and none of them seemed to mind. Here you are with a nice back and not a bad-looking face and this seat is plenty wide. . . ."

"But there are men all around us." Dirk grabbed at straws, any excuse. The truth was he was having a little trouble. Her eyes—those damn eyes. And he kept thinking of Margaret, and the sun was on them.

The rest of the day ground on. She seemed to spend a good part of the time crawling on him—much to the amusement of men who happened to be walking nearby. It seemed like one moment she would be on his back, chewing on his neck, the next tonguing his ear again, or sticking her finger in his mouth.

Puberty, Dirk thought, sure takes some

women funny. He used most of a linen bag of water himself, twice pouring it on his head to cool down, and hoped, prayed, that they would get into Central City soon and he would not have to spend the night with her.

Which was of course a futile hope. Darkness caught them where the canyons flattened out into a wide area, still a short day's pull from Central City, and the team was dragged to nothing and he had to stop. He could not have kept going at night at any rate. They would have fallen off the edge in the dark and dropped into the river. He pulled well away from the river and off the trail and road, around in back of some boulders that were large enough to hide a house, and unhooked the team.

He thought they would have to spend another cold night with no fire but Sam proved to be an agile climber. Up a near vertical face next to where they stopped she scrabbled to a ledge that held some dead pine. She threw the wood down and Dirk started a fire and in a short time they had beans cooking with cut chunks of bacon in them. She produced some salt from a small cloth sack in her pocket and they set the beans to simmer, adding a piece of wood now and then to keep them hot.

By then it was hard dark and in the glow from the fire Dirk pulled the bedrolls from the wagon and put them on the ground. Four feet apart.

"What are you doing?" She was sitting by the fire and had taken her hat off and the flames caught her hair and her eyes again. The eyes. What Dirk thought of now as the Margaret eyes. The fire showed the small flecks and they almost glowed.

"Getting the bedrolls ready."

"Won't need but one."

"No." Dirk shook his head, pointed at her roll—which was meager enough. Tattered and worn. "You sleep over there. I sleep here, by the wagon. I have to be ready in case somebody comes. . . ."

"Easier to stay warm if there's two in a bedroll. Pa, he won't let me because he says it's not natural, but you ain't Pa and we might as well be warm. . . ."

Dirk again shook his head but said no more and went ahead and set the rolls apart. He put hers near the fire and his own back, almost under the wagon. He didn't figure to sleep much—the night before had taught him that—and if he lay back in the shadow of the wagon it might give him a little extra cover if somebody came up on them.

The beans would not be done for at least two hours. Belly beans cooked slow. And hungry as he was he didn't feel it was right to eat the berries. He gave Sam some hard candy from the sack Holtzer had bought—she was delighted with it—and they settled in for the night.

Briefly.

Initially he forced her to stay in her own bed, and Sam seemed to give in. Dirk settled into his own roll to rest until the beans were done but no sooner had he settled in than he sensed movement and saw her come from her bedroll to his.

She slipped silently in beside him, wrapped herself around him—he was silent all the while, wondering why he didn't say anything. Wondering why he thought only of Margaret. Wondering why his body was so weak.

"See?" she said. "It's warmer, ain't it?"

Then she clamped her mouth to his and by that time he was past any kind of resolve. Once or twice in the night he thought he called the name of Margaret, but couldn't be sure.

Couldn't be sure of anything. He did not eat the beans, did not get much sleep, did not guard the berries, did nothing but stay alive as Sam took her puberty out on him with a vengeance, and when dawn finally cracked and he knew it was time to get up and get the team going he couldn't.

Couldn't move his legs.

Even his eyelids were tired.

Sam got a fire going and brought him a cup of fresh coffee—his first in three days—and then harnessed the team, and all the while he was still sitting under the wagon, sipping coffee. God, he thought, how can I face her father? What am I? No willpower, no control. Just like an animal. A very tired animal. A dead animal.

She was perky and bright and as full of energy as he was tired, and he did not fully awaken until he was up in the wagon and they had settled into pulling toward Central City.

"You don't talk much in the morning, do you?" She had tucked her hair back under her hat but it no longer kept him from seeing the beauty of her.

"I . . . don't have much to say."

"I thought maybe that last time was too much for you. Some men can go longer. . . ."

"Oh?"

"Well, some not so long, either. You was about in the middle."

"Thank you."

"You're welcome." She sighed, thinking. "You remind me of a boy I met back in Hastings. He was kind of shy and took some coaxing but once he got going he wasn't so bad. . . ."

"Sam."

"What?"

"I don't think you have to tell me about other men. Let's just ride quiet for a while, all right?"

"Oh. Sure." She shrugged. "I just thought it

would help you to know that there's others about like you. I'll keep quiet."

And she was as good as her word. For the rest of the morning and into early afternoon they rode in silence.

Until they rounded a bend in the river and there was Central City and Dirk could not believe what he saw.

CHAPTER

7

"GOD," Sam said, "it's like somebody kicked the top off an anthill."

And it was. Exactly.

The town was a ramshackle collection of plank buildings and tents with a few brick buildings thrown in and men.

Thousands of men.

They were crawling all over the place, jammed together shoulder to shoulder moving down the streets, across the streets, being thrown out of the seemingly dozens of saloons, moving and jumping and running and sober and drunk and yelling men.

"I ain't never seen or heard of anything like this," Sam said. Her voice was soft, awed. "You couldn't handle them all in a year. It's like the stockyards back in Kansas."

Dirk looked at her but said nothing. If last night hadn't taken the edge off her he guessed nothing would. Not even this.

One man caught his eye. The plank saloons—some covered with nailed-down tarps, others just boards—were pretty much built wall to wall, so that the wall in one saloon was the same wall in another. A fire would sweep through in moments.

But between two particular saloons there was a slight gap—perhaps two feet. And a man had set up housekeeping in the opening. He had arranged a couple of boards to make a small roof, covered it with a rag of canvas, and had a bedroll and a couple of pots back under the shelter. He was sitting in the opening, leaning against one wall.

Stone dead.

Dirk had seen enough death to know it. He was dead and by the looks of him had died of starvation and he'd heard of that as well. Bodies in the streets and men dying for want of food. But he hadn't believed it. Until now.

And nobody cared.

Others walked past the body as if it weren't there, stepped over the legs—which stuck out a little in the walkway. How could they stand the smell? These hot days the body would go off fast. The flies would be at it. And nobody seemed to care.

Like the war.

Madness. Crazy. Just like the war.

"There's Pa!" Sam hit him on the back. She had not seen the dead man—Dirk supposed because she was more inclined to the living ones—and in her excitement her blow almost took Dirk off the seat.

"Over there—by that brick building. See him waving at us?"

It was hard to miss him. There he was, Abe Lincoln, standing head and shoulders above the moving men, waving at them.

Dirk angled the team across the press of men in the main street. They had become better, the horses, but were still tired. The grade had increased as they pulled close to town and the weight had dragged them down. So it took them several minutes to pull ahead and across and Dirk had time to wonder why he wasn't seeing any fliers, or why there weren't any men ready to buy berries. He'd heard stories about selling potatoes in the diggings in California where men fought over single small potatoes with knives. Food was worth more than gold. And yet not a man seemed to care that they were there.

The team stopped in front of Ben, who was smiling and still waving.

Dirk noticed now that he wasn't alone. With him, standing on the boardwalk in front of the bank—as the brick building proved to be—was a fat man in a suit. He was wearing a linen duster that went to the ground—probably to protect his suit from the street dust. It was open in the front as well as his coat and Dirk could see a gold chain and fob that went across the expanse of his belly. In back of him Dirk could now see that there were three men—three big men—who were standing against the wall. They seemed to be waiting.

"You made good time," Ben said and the man next to him—clearly the banker—pulled his watch and checked it as if to emphasize Ben's statement.

Dirk nodded. "We had to stop for the night...." He let it trail off, remembering Sam and the night, hoping he didn't look too guilty.

But if Ben wondered about the night it didn't show.

"This is Burdock. Evan Burdock. He is the president and owner of the Central City State and Federal Bank." Ben gestured widely to the building in back of him. "And he has taken care of our problem for us."

"I didn't know we had a problem," Dirk said. He stood in the seat and stretched, let his hand fall next to the gun. He did not particularly like bankers and felt ill at ease. He wished the three men weren't there—noticed now that they were all armed, while most of the miners weren't—and that they didn't look like strangers to fighting. One of them had a nose that looked like it had been pushed all over his face before it settled down. "We've just got some berries to sell and I aim to sell them."

Burdock cleared his throat and stepped forward on the boardwalk. "That's just it, Mr. . . ."

"Prine," Dirk said. "Duncan Prine."

"That's just it, Mr. Prine," he repeated. "The berries are already sold. You sent your man forward and he concluded the deal for you."

"Now wait a minute. He's not 'my man,' and he wasn't supposed to do anything but get it all set up for the sale. He had no right to sell the berries. . . ."

"For five thousand dollars," Burdock interrupted.

Dirk stared at him.

"Cash."

"Well. . . ." Dirk said. Five thousand dollars—not so bad. The uneasy feeling left him. Five thousand was a thousand more than Holtzer hoped to get. "Well."

Burdock smiled. "Why don't you come in the bank and we'll close the deal. I have a lot of work to do. Oh, it's assumed that for five thousand I will get the team and wagon as well."

Dirk relaxed and nodded. "Sure." He'd been

wrong so many times in his hunches and all this seemed to be aboveboard.

He swung off the wagon and onto the boardwalk. His legs were still weak from the night before but he hid it and followed Ben and Burdock into the bank.

There Burdock turned. "Do you want payment in gold coins or dust?"

"I think coins," Dirk answered. He didn't know much about gold and the dust could be diluted with lead and he wouldn't know it. "Yes. Gold coins."

Inside the bank it was dark and cooler than out in the sun. There was a wooden barrier with two tellers' cages halfway across the room and in back Dirk could see the vault. One man, wearing glasses, was in the teller's cage and he looked up from counting when the men walked in but went back to work immediately with a look from Burdock.

The bank president walked around the barrier and into an office in the rear, next to the vault, motioning for Dirk and Ben and Sam to follow him.

Inside the office there was a large desk—it looked to be made of walnut—and a shiny brass oil lamp hanging from the ceiling. Everything, Dirk thought, everything stank of money. Hell, I could live two months off that lamp alone.

He pushed the thought away, not sure why

he was feeling so proddy. Everything was open and honest so far.

Burdock wasted no time. As soon as they were seated he went to the door and called to one of the tellers.

"William, bring five thousand in fifty-dollar gold pieces from the vault, will you? With one of those carrying bags?"

While they were waiting Burdock asked about their trip up, chatted about the weather, expressed his condolences for Holtzer and the way he died.

"It's horrible, how these camps attract low men. Murder, robbery, and worse. I hear stories, awful stories... just terrible. Just last week they found a man nailed to the side of his cabin with a log spike through his head—in one ear and out the other." He paused, seemed to be thinking. "It's not my place to ask, Mr. Prine, but how do you intend handling this gold?"

"Why?" Dirk's mistrust of bankers surfaced again. All the way back to his father's farm in Pennsylvania. Bankers were not to be trusted. It never rained when you needed it and bankers were not to be trusted.

"It's a matter of risk. Banks deal in risk and this seems to be a risky business. If you just take off back down the trail with one hundred fifty-dollar gold pieces you may have trouble. There are hard men and long riders on that track who would kill you for your clothing, let alone all that money."

Dirk waited.

"It is my understanding that you wish to send the money back to this man's family in Europe."

Dirk looked at Ben. He had mentioned it while riding in the wagon and apparently Ben had told the banker.

Burdock cleared his throat again. "It would be much simpler for you to send a bank draft. I could give you a certified draft for five thousand dollars good anywhere in the world and you could simply mail it to Europe. It would be much easier and safer to handle than gold."

In fact this was exactly what Dirk had thought of doing. But from Denver. He thought to find a large bank in Denver—when dealing with banks he had heard it was better to use the large ones—and send a draft.

But not here.

Not from this man.

"I'll just take the gold."

"As you wish, of course. I was just trying to ease the risk." There was a flicker of something there, some hard edge came into his eyes and moved away, was pushed away. There and gone as Burdock controlled it, and Dirk thought this is the main bull in this pasture and he likes to have his way, doesn't like to be pushed.

The teller came in then with a canvas bag and Burdock emptied the contents gently on the desk.

"Jesus Christ." Sam had been uncharacteristically quiet the whole time and she swore almost as a prayer.

Dirk felt the same way. He'd never seen so much money in one place at one time in his life. One hundred fifty-dollar gold pieces lay in a pile on the desk.

Burdock counted them and arranged them in ten neat piles of ten each.

Dirk nodded. He took two of them and handed them to Ben.

He took another and handed it to Sam, half smiling as he remembered the night. For services rendered, he thought. Maybe she should pay me. She must have been thinking along the same lines because she smiled back at him and the corners of her eyes were alive with devilment.

He took four for himself and put them in his pocket. The two hundred dollars Holtzer had agreed to pay him.

The rest he put back in the sack.

"I thank you," Burdock said, standing. "A good business deal is where everybody comes out ahead and this one seems to be that way."

"What are you going to do with the berries?" Dirk asked.

"Why sell them," Burdock said. "Of course. This afternoon at a public auction. And hope I make a profit. Why don't you come and watch?"

Dirk thought a moment. He wanted to get back to Denver but he also wanted to see the diggings. He could wait and leave tomorrow.

"You can leave the gold here until you're ready to leave," Burdock said. "I assure you it will be safe."

Dirk hesitated only a moment. He'd been wrong all along about this man and any doubt he had was probably wrong as well. At length he nodded. "I'll leave tomorrow."

"Fine. Just see the teller out front and he'll give you a receipt for the gold."

"Is there anywhere in town where a man can find a good meal?" Dirk had eaten cold beans and bacon for breakfast in the morning with his coffee after the night's activities but he longed for meat and potatoes.

Burdock nodded. "Wing's place, across the street, but it will shock you. . . ."

"What do you mean?"

"You'll see. But the food is good."

They went out of the bank and across the street to a small cafe nailed up between two saloon tents.

There was a line, of sorts. Perhaps more like a bunch. Men were packed around the walls waiting to get to the tables. At the tables more men sat eating. Not talking, not drinking, not salting nor peppering their food nor scratching nor farting nor belching nor even breathing much.

They were eating.

On the tables were metal pie pans nailed down to the plank surface, each with a galvanized roofing nail through the center. One dozen to a table, six down each side, and next to each plate was a large enamel spoon tied with a piece of cord to a nail near the plate.

As Dirk and Ben and Sam watched, twelve men sat to the nearest table, grabbed spoons, and a short Chinese man came out of the kitchen carrying a large steel pot and a ladle. He slopped a dipper full of stew on each plate—faster than Dirk had seen some men slop hogs and with about the same neatness—then turned and went back into the kitchen.

A Chinese woman sat with a small table next to the door and took money from men as they came in.

On the wall next to the menu placard was another sign that said:

ALL FOOD MUST BE DONE IN FIVE MINUTES FROM THE TIME YOU SIT DOWN. BE SURE TO LICK SPOON CLEAN.

As each table was done the men left—some licking not just the spoon but the pie pan as well—and a new mob sat down.

"I'm suddenly not very hungry," Ben said.

"I ain't ever going to be able to eat stew again," Sam said.

Dirk nodded. "I guess we can go out of town and make a fire and eat some beans and bacon. Then I guess I'll head on back down to Denver."

"I thought you wanted to see the diggings," Ben said as they left the cafe and walked out into the sun.

"I've seen enough."

"I think we'll stay a little and see if we can work a claim. There so much . . . energy here. So much raw energy."

"And men," Sam put in. "Lots of men."

Dirk looked at her and away when she smiled. Like a cat, he thought. She smiles like a cat. About to eat a mouse. He almost felt sorry for the miners.

Across the street at the bank there was already a large crowd of men forming around the wagon. The crowd was growing fast and the three men who had first checked the load for the banker were on top of the wagon. Two of them held pick handles and one had a double-barrel shotgun and they looked ready to use the weapons if anybody touched the wagon.

As they watched Burdock came out of the

bank. He was wearing a flat brim black hat and smoking a cigar and jerked his vest down a bit, looked up at the sun, and spit into the dirt.

"He's going to start the auction," Ben said. "He's not going to wait until the afternoon. He's doing it right now."

"Before the berries spoil," Sam said.

Dirk watched. Still stunned from the cafe prices and the way men were fed he found that he couldn't believe almost everything he saw. Money, literally, meant nothing. Either men had it, and didn't care how much they spent for anything they bought, or they had nothing and starved to death like the man between the two buildings. He looked and saw that somebody had taken the body away.

By now word had spread like fire through the town and there was a large mob around the wagon that spilled out into the street and covered most of the length of the block.

I'll stay for this, he thought, and get the hell out. Something about it, everything about it sickened him. The greed, the stink of greed was in everything.

When the mob was jammed so tightly that a man could pass out without falling down Burdock climbed up on the wagon and held up a small wooden box—one-pound box of strawberries.

An almost reverent hush fell over the men.

"I'm auctioning this wagon load of strawberries either by the one-pound box or the whole lot. What am I bid per pound?"

"Three dollars!" one man yelled, starting the bidding. "Per pound, for the lot. And another four hundred for the wagon and team."

It was the last coherent sound. The bidding was less an auction than a voice war. Men yelled, screamed, tore at each other to get to the front of the crowd to bid and bid again. Inside seconds it went to five, six, and then seven dollars a box. Then eight.

And nine.

Dirk caught himself holding his breath. It was madness, just madness. Nine dollars a box, by the lot. Seventy-two hundred dollars. Almost twenty years' wages.

And nine and a half.

And, finally, ten dollars a box.

Eight thousand dollars.

You could hire a man for forty a month and work him twelve hours a day, seven days a week on a cow pony and these men were willing to pay ten dollars a pound for strawberries.

And that was it. Ten dollars a pound for the whole lot and an extra fifteen hundred for the wagon and team.

Eleven thousand five hundred dollars for something not worth five hundred dollars in St. Louis.

Dirk turned away.

But it wasn't over yet. The ice inside the sawdust had been melting since they put it in down in Denver and was draining out of the tailgate of the wagon.

Juice from the berries had mixed in with the melting ice and the stream had a faint red color.

Somebody had put a bucket beneath the stream—little more than a trickle—and the man who bought the wagon and berries, after paying Burdock in gold in front of the wagon and team, turned around and auctioned the juice off for thirty dollars a bucket.

And the man who bought the juice yelled that he would be selling strawberry-flavored skull buster in two days for fifteen dollars a jug.

And then, finally, it was done.

Dirk had a moment of regret, thinking that Holtzer could have made much more money if Dirk had auctioned the berries himself. But Holtzer had stated that he expected four thousand and Dirk had done better than that rate. The fact that Burdock had turned it around and made more than double in half an hour didn't matter. Holtzer's family would still get a tidy amount of money.

He shook his head and started toward the bay. The horse had been tied to the hitch rail in front of the bank throughout all the auction and was jammed in tightly still with men. They were all trying to buy the boxes from the buyer, one at a time, and Dirk had to push them aside to reach the horse.

Ben and Sam started to follow but Ben stopped. "If you're heading back I guess we might as well part company here. . . ."

Dirk turned. He had come to like the tall man—and more than like the daughter—but he wanted out of the diggings now. He'd seen, smelled enough. He could see nothing good about it.

They shook hands and Sam surprised him by standing on tiptoe to kiss him demurely on the cheek. He expected to feel her tongue in his ear but she looked down shyly and smiled.

"I'll miss you," she whispered and Dirk answered the smile. With all these men it wasn't likely. But he would probably miss her for a while.

He turned and went into the bank and got the sack of gold eagles, tied them in his saddlebags, and started out of town.

He was at the edge, heading back down toward Denver on the trail—against the traffic—when he realized that the saddlebag he'd put the gold in had been empty. Somebody had stolen the beans and bacon.

He debated riding back into town to buy some more and turned the bay, then decided against it. Beans were probably a hundred dollars a pound and bacon worse. He could ride lean to Denver. On the bay it shouldn't take more than a night ride and part of a day.

He turned back, the bay tossing his head in irritation at the indecision.

Just before he turned he looked at the bank again and saw Burdock talking to the three men who had helped him with the wagon.

They were looking at him.

CHAPTER

THE ride down was much different from the ride up. The bay, fresh from having not been ridden in close on a week, was full of it and wanted to run. There was too much traffic on the road to let him out, but when Dirk saw a clear space for a bit he'd turn the big horse loose and try to get a sweat on him.

Time went fast. He stopped just at dark to water the horse and sip some for himself. In his shirt pocket he found two pieces of hard candy and he sucked on one for close to an hour as the sun went down and he made his way away from the diggings.

It marveled him that he'd thought he wanted to see them, to be in them, and he couldn't help thinking of them, of all that he'd seen as he rode. In fact the whole business with the berries was a mystery to him; almost a great show. A snake-oil show. So many men pushing and fighting and shoving just for strawberries.

They'd eat them in a minute and they'd be gone, all completely gone. Like the whores. He'd seen them in the upper windows of the buildings, the whores that worked the miners, and had heard one man say to another that one of them—a whore named Maggie—charged a hundred dollars for one time. A hundred dollars.

And it would be gone in a minute.

Which made him think naturally of Sam, who was of course not a whore but prompted some of the same feelings and—he was sure—damn near killed him. His legs still felt weak.

Because his mind was lost on Sam and the diggings, rolling along in loose thoughts, he did not notice that shapes had appeared in the darkness to his left front. And when he saw them he thought they might be shadows. There was no moon and in the starlight it was difficult to see.

Until one of the shadows moved and he realized he was looking at men, three men sitting on horses.

He reined in, pulled the bay's head around to the right, and it saved his life.

The darkness was split suddenly with white light, flashing light and the thunderous sound of a double-barrel shotgun going off, and he saw in the quick light three men facing him, just shapes, really, and the light went out.

Because he'd pulled the bay's head around the horse took most of the charge from the two barrels in the neck and head. Dirk felt something rip across the front of his chest, pulling at his shirt, and knew he was hit but most of it was absorbed by the bay.

It killed the horse instantly. So fast that for a part of a second he stood, his legs locked. In that second Dirk pulled at his gun, or tried to, but when the bay pitched forward he dropped the gun. His feet were still jammed into the stirrups and he fought to get loose, away.

"Goddammit, you missed! Get something in the son of a bitch. Burdock said kill him. We half kill our horses getting ahead of him and you miss. . . ."

Voices.

He thought he knew them, had heard them, but it didn't matter.

His leg was caught under the bay. Dirk kicked, pulled, swore. They would shoot again in a moment and they couldn't miss and he didn't have a gun, didn't have a chance.

His leg came free, pulled out of the boot. He had to get away. He half rose, scrabbled, clawed away from the horse, and there was another explosion.

Huge.

A ball of flame this time that somehow seemed to roll over him, around him, through him. He felt the charge—it must have been both barrels again—take him at an angle across the back, in the neck, driving him forward. It was a staggering blow, a sledgehammer blow that drove him forward and down and he knew he was dead.

Knew it.

He could not live from such a hit. Nothing could live. But his brain didn't stop, didn't turn off. He felt the shock come and smelled his death but his head didn't stop and it made his legs move, pushing him along the ground on his hands and knees away, away from the men and the gun. The white rolling thunder of the shotgun.

Away toward the edge of the river. He could smell-hear the river below and to the right and did not think, did nothing but shove along the ground like an animal.

They would shoot again as soon as they reloaded. Shoot him and kill him if he wasn't dead already.

He had to make the river. If he could get there, maybe he could get away.

Suddenly everything fell away. His hand

came down on air and his feet pushed him over, over the edge to fall down the rock face, bouncing when he hit, spinning end over end until he hit the water.

Still alive somehow.

Bleeding and blown apart but still alive.

He heard two more shots, or thought he heard them, then the white water took him, roared with him downstream, and he fought to stay on top and was clawing at it when the boulders caught him, slammed him from side to side like a wood chip, and in the pain he lost his thinking and remembered nothing after that.

Nothing.

CHAPTER 9

FLOWERS and sun.

He remembered them from when he was a boy on the farm in Pennsylvania. Before the war. There had been flowers and sun and he went in back of the barn to look for mushrooms with Delia, the girl from the next farm. They sought puffballs in the pasture, to fry in white butter with salt and pepper. There hadn't been any puffballs but they had gone below the line of trees in the back pasture and there had been flowers and the warm sun and Delia had set herself by the rail fence and picked some flowers to hold against her cheek.

"See? They make me lavender, don't they, Duncan?"

And Dirk—who had been Duncan then—

nodded and thought he'd never seen anything so beautiful and tried to steal a kiss and maybe more than a kiss because his voice had changed and he thought of little else.

But Delia had laughed and pushed him away and jumped to run away, laughing.

"See—there's some color here now."

Which he thought was also Delia's voice but it was harsh, a low voice. Not a girl but a woman, an old woman, and he wondered how Delia could have gotten old without his knowing.

He tried to hold the picture of the pasture and the sun and the flowers but it slipped, slipped and moved away like smoke, and his eyes opened.

Pain.

It started in his back and neck and worked around to the front somehow so that he wanted to scream, cry and scream but it was so intense, so hot and burning that he could not make any sound but a whine.

"If you can understand me lay still, goddammit. You look like you stuck your head in a goddamn mill grinder and I got to clean it out."

It was the woman's voice again, raspy and low. Dirk was lying on his face on a board surface of some kind—maybe a floor, he couldn't be sure—and she seemed to be digging in his back.

With what felt like a hot poker.

"Don't. . . ." He tried to tell her to stop. The pain was tearing him apart.

"Have to dig for it. They used buckshot on you and it took the shirt in with it. Shit, you got more rags inside than you got out. With all that in you it'll be lucky if you don't mortify and die."

He couldn't stand the pain and his brain slipped away again, back to the barn and pasture and Delia.

Cornflower hair and freckles across her nose, teasing and laughing and part of the summer sun and the pasture and he loved her. He could stay with her there forever with the sounds of birds singing and a cowbell clanging and nothing to think of, nothing to think of but. . . .

His eyes opened again.

She was jerking at something now, jerking at his back so hard it lifted his chest off the floor.

"Goddamn rags, they're in under things. Lord, I hate a shotgun."

And he went under again.

Different this time, all different. He saw his father. Dirk was young and it was before his father was gone. His father was sewing on a harness, his strong hands pushing the awl through for the waxed thread. He looked up and smiled at Dirk, a pleasant smile. The only smile Dirk ever remembered and he came up again.

The old woman seemed to be done. He was lying in a puddle of blood on the floor and it seemed to be midday. The sun was high and hot and he heard a swarm of flies, drawn by the blood and the wound. The sound of war. Flies. God, they must love war. Death. Wounds.

He could not move.

Not any part of him except his eyelids. He tried to make a sound but could do nothing but croak. His throat was dry, dry and woody.

"Don't talk. Don't try to do nothing."

A pair of boots came into his vision, standing in the blood. They were heavy miner's boots, thick leather, meant to last. He saw a pair of jeans going up from the boots but could not see higher than the knee.

It was the same voice, the old woman's voice.

"I'm afraid to move you. I think you might die anyways, but if I move you I *know* you'll die. Your back ain't nothing but pig slop, by the looks of it. . . ."

"Wat . . . water."

She chuckled—gravel on tin. A grating sound. "Thirsty, are you? I thought you'd never want to drink again. Shit, I pumped most of a river out of you."

The problem was with the angle of his head he couldn't drink, his mouth down and to the side. She tried to pour from a dipper into his mouth but most of it ran into the puddle on the floor.

"Don't drink from the puddle," she said. "It's blood and garbage from your back and worse, you been pissing in it. Just wait, I'll get the powder funnel, maybe it will work."

She was gone a minute—it seemed a week—and returned to stick a funnel in his mouth. It tasted of black powder and tin.

"I use it for pouring powder in holes to blast, but it should work."

She poured some water through it and some of it went into his mouth. He swallowed gratefully, got perhaps a cup of it down, and threw up on the floor.

"Jesus," she said—he'd still only seen the boots and her hands on the funnel, which looked like a man's hands. "Ain't you the sick pup? You rest and I'll try some more later."

Dirk slipped away again, as if following orders.

He could not be sure how long he was under this time. It was dark when he came to again, dark enough so that the woman had lighted an oil lantern.

He must have moved in his sleep, or unconsciousness, or she may have moved his head, because he could see higher now. The lantern was sitting on a crude table along a plank wall and the woman was sitting at the table.

She was old, but not as old as her voice sounded. She sounded sixty or seventy, but she didn't look much over forty-five or fifty. It was hard to make her features out. The lantern threw less light than a table lamp and that was blocked by the handles on the sides.

She had a long face, he could see that much, and gray hair tied back in a stream that hung down her back over her canvas jacket. She wore rough miner's clothes—jeans and work shirt and jacket.

Dirk saw all this without moving his head, studying her in silence. And he realized suddenly that he *couldn't* move his head.

Terror took him. One of his worst fears of the war was that he could be hit either in the groin or back and be paralyzed.

What did the docs say? Oh, yeah, move your feet. If you could move your feet it meant you were all right.

He tried and did not feel them move, felt nothing. But he heard a scraping sound and knew his toe was moving and felt huge relief. To die was one thing, but to live without being able to move, to be paralyzed—God.

The woman heard the movement as well and stood from the table to walk over to him. As she moved she changed the angle and he could no longer see her face.

"So you're awake," she said, her voice raking. It reminded him of something awful, something he couldn't at first place until he thought of the sound of a shovel being jammed into dirt and hitting a rock.

That sound.

"Where . . . am . . . I?" He thought he was talking but all that came out was a rasp. Almost as bad as hers.

She put the funnel in his mouth again and he drank a little water. This time he held it down.

"Where am I?" he repeated.

"You're at my mine, that's where you are." She squatted down next to him and he saw her face and was surprised to see that it was beautiful. Or had been. There were wrinkles and age showing but the dimness hid much of them and she had brown eyes that lifted well at the corners and laugh lines at the sides. She must have once been the prettiest girl in the county.

"Where is your mine?"

"I'm about eleven miles below Central City, maybe eight miles from where the road to Denver curves away from the river."

Eight miles, he thought. I swam eight miles? No, more like bounced eight miles. From rock to rock. "That's where I got in the river. About where the road moves away and heads for Denver. I think."

She nodded. "I thought as much. Or near there. There's not much country between here and there where you could have got into the water. It's all rock canyons and boulders."

"I need to go. . . ."

"You've been going right along—the floor's a mess."

"No. The other one." It tore at him to ask but he had no choice. "Could you drop my pants and roll me over?"

"Nope. I mean I can maybe get your pants down but if I roll you it will kill you sure. There's broken bones in there and I'm afraid they'll take your lung."

"Then that—drop the pants."

Dirk was mortified and when he was done she cleaned him and pulled his pants up and all the while he was so embarrassed he wished he could die, wished he had died.

"It ain't much," she said, guessing what he felt. "I had me two boys and it's just like diapers. Don't fret."

"How long have I been here?" He changed the subject.

"Two, no, three days now. You floated by and I thought you were dead. I was working a cradle down by the river, looking for dust, and you come by like a rotten log. I was going to let you go on by—I get a body every three or four days past here—but you moved your arm and I thought I'd better pull you in. That was three days ago."

"I can't move very well."

"Move—hell, I can't believe you're alive. Speaking of that, I don't mean to sound grim but is there somebody you want that money sent to if you don't make it?"

"What money?" For a second he thought of the gold coins from the bank but they had been in the saddlebags and had stayed with the bay. And the men.

The goddamn men. He tried to remember some of what had happened and couldn't. Not a word, not a sound, not an action. He just remembered some men and the rolling cloud of light and the slam of being hit and falling in the river. Then nothing. Not a thing.

"You had two hundred dollars in your pocket—is there some place you want that sent if you don't make it?"

Oh, yes, he'd taken his pay out of the coins. That money. "You can keep it. If I don't make it."

"Well, thanks, but I ain't done that much."

"Just keep it."

"If you don't make it."

"Yes."

"You want to try some soup?" It was her turn

to change the subject. "You've got to try eating. You lost most of the blood in your body, the way it looks."

He nodded, or tried to nod, or thought he tried to nod. At any rate she understood and brought a bowl and a spoon and put the funnel in his mouth once more and poured soup so hot it felt like molten lead.

He jerked back and the sudden movement made the pain come roaring out of his shoulder again and the red wave settled on his brain once more.

CHAPTER

HE was in a different place.

When his eyes opened this time he saw that he had moved. He was still in the cabin but against the wall opposite the door, lying sideways. He could see where he'd lain. There was a large wet place—she must have used buckets of water from the river to slosh the muck out.

He was looking outside, straight through the open door, and he could see it was daylight again—he could not guess the time of day. The river was slightly below the level of the door, but he could see the far shore and though the land seemed to be fairly level by the cabin it was still rolling by at a good clip.

The pain in his back had subsided to an angry

rawness. The woman was nowhere to be seen or heard and he had to piss again.

He looked down and she had provided a can and he used it—or tried to. But he had to move with such agonizing slowness—grateful that his arms *could* move—that he was about to burst before he could roll slightly and hit the can.

When he did accomplish it he felt inordinately proud, then had to smile at himself.

Proud of being able to piss in a can.

He forced his mind to relax. He was lucky to be alive, and would be damn lucky if he stayed alive, let alone able to piss.

Two things hit him. He was unbelievably thirsty and so hungry he felt like he could eat horse shit if it had gravy on it.

He could swivel his head slightly, if he did it slowly. There were some damaged cords in his neck and they seemed to saw at something when he moved, but if he did it slowly enough he could look around.

She must have been planning on being gone awhile because she had put a small lard pail of water near his head with a dipper next to it and a bowl of something covered with a dirty cloth.

Dirk moved his left arm slowly, let his fingers pull the arm across the floor until his hand reached the lard pail. He pulled it toward him and after what seemed like years of effort he moved a dipperful of water to his mouth and drank.

It was warm—she must have been gone some time—but it tasted sweet and wonderful, better than anything he'd ever tasted—and he drank several dippers.

Then he looked to the bowl. He moved the rag off the top and found soup with a spoon in it. As soon as he moved the rags the flies found it—rose from his back in a hissing drone—and he had to wave his hand over it. It was awkward because he could only use his left arm, lying on his face, but he would wave and eat a spoonful, then wave and eat another and was doing that—not even minding the flies—when she walked in.

"You found the soup, eh? Good." She clumped through the door in her miner's boots and stood by the table, taking a carbide lamp off her head. "I had to work in the hole and blow a line into a new vein. Or where I thought there was a new vein. So I left the soup."

He put the spoon down, finished. "What part of the day is it?"

She laughed. "Which day? You've been here a week now. Seems like when you go down, you go down long. I thought this last time you were going to die but you just keep clawing back up."

A week. Jesus, he thought, I've been lying

here a week, not moving. "I don't even know your name."

Another laugh. "It's Carmen. That's a joke, isn't it? Carmen Belser. Carmen the miner."

"I'm Dirk—Duncan by birth, Dirk to friends. Dirk Prine." He wanted to say more, to thank her, but no words came. It seemed like an effort just to speak and when he took a breath to make words something stretched in his back and hurt like hell. He had to be slow, slow and careful about everything he did.

She took her heavy jacket off and draped it on a nail on the wall. "Well, Dirk Prine, would you like to eat something better than soup?"

He nodded. "How did you move me?"

"That was on the third, no, fourth day. I slid a plank under you and dragged you sideways to the wall. I wasn't sure if it would kill you or not but you was lying there in that muck and I had to clean it. Seems to have worked out, doesn't it?"

He nodded again. Each time he moved it became easier but his back felt tight, wrong somehow.

"I've got some bacon," she said, "and beans. Suit you?"

"Fine." He wanted to ask about his back, ask her what was going on back there but was half afraid to. Finally he screwed up his courage. "How does my back look?"

She had bacon on the table and was cutting chunks of it to put in the beans to cook and she paused, the knife in the air. "Like hell. How do you think it looks?"

"It feels . . . funny. Tight or something."

She nodded. A strand of hair had come from in back of her ear and she pushed it away with the back of her hand. A little girl's gesture. When it fell back she blew at it and finally stuck it in back of her ear with a greasy finger. "That's all scab. It's healing but it's all scab and that's why it's tight. I've tried to change the bandage when I could but I didn't have much cloth so I had to use it over. Boil it and use it again."

All this, he thought, for me. For something floating down the goddamn river. Another body. And she did all this. "I never said thank you."

"You aren't over it yet," she said. "I've never seen anything like it. They used double-ought buck on you—I found some still in your back—and it went across kind of sideways. It made a right mess of you, a right mess. The skin was torn in long strips and I had to piece it back together like weaving and how come it didn't mortify I'll never know. But it don't stink much and seems to be knitting back together."

All the time she was speaking she was cutting chunks of bacon and she dropped them in an iron pot with pinto beans and put them on a stove.

She lit the stove expertly, chopping kindling with an axe by the door, and Dirk felt the heat from the stove fill the small room.

He looked around the cabin for the first time. There were two bunks near the wall to the right as you came in the door—he paused at seeing the two bunks—and the stove and some wooden dynamite boxes stacked sideways full of odds and ends of gear.

A miner's shack.

Eight miles down a river where there were no roads. This old woman working a mine, alone.

It didn't make a lot of sense to him.

"If it isn't wrong to ask," he said, "how come you be here?"

She turned from the stove. "What you really mean is how come I'm alone, isn't it?"

"No . . . well, yes. I guess. But I don't mean to pry where I'm not wanted. Just curious."

"Let me finish chores and we'll talk a bit. . . ."

She turned away and went outside and Dirk lay back. He closed his eyes and slipped away once more. But it was only light dozing, a comfort, a warm comfort.

CHAPTER 11

"I was a whore on the riverboats working from New Orleans up to St. Louis."

She said it matter-of-factly, with no shame. The beans had cooked, and the bacon—Dirk had sworn more than once after the army that he would never eat beans and bacon again and yet here he was, stuffing them down. She had helped him to prop his front up a bit with some boards and sacking for padding and while doing it he found that he could crawl.

It was slow work. He could only move his hands about six inches at a time. But it allowed him some movement and he could go outside to piss. Like a dog, he thought, on all fours—except that he couldn't lift his leg.

An animal.

Now they were sitting, or she was sitting and he was leaning, eating beans and bacon and talking and she was saying what it was like to be a whore.

"It was elegant," she said. "Or at least what I did. There was trash on the boats—in fact it was mostly trash on the boats. The worst was the buffalo hunters. God damn, they smelled bad. But I didn't cater to them, or to the soldiers, who were almost as bad." She ate a spoonful of beans and Dirk did the same. The bacon had salted them and the pork taste mixed with the beans and it tasted better than steak to him. He had never been so hungry and thought he could eat all night, and would have, if the worry about throwing it up hadn't been there.

"I ran with the gamblers." She laughed. "At least the ones who won. I cost too much for the losers. Look at me"—she stood from the table suddenly, held her coat out—"look here—it was a hundred dollars a night for this. When buffalo girls and sluts were selling it for fifty cents and a dollar, I got a hundred a night and turned many a man down. Can you believe it?"

The truth was that Dirk *could* believe it. Even now, in miner's clothes and her age on her, she was beautiful; stood well and straight. Her face caught the light, her eyes and face and he could well believe men would have spent a hundred a night for her.

She sat again to the table. "But a whore has got to be young. You can't be an old whore. You can be a dead whore, a retired whore, but you can't be an old one. There's too many young ones coming along and a man will always choose a young one over an old one. . . ."

Not always, Dirk thought. But he didn't say anything.

"It was elegant," she said, smiling, remembering. "The boats were elegant. Red velvet and crystal and servants. I had a bed on one boat—she was called the H. Jackson, out of Memphis—I had a bed on her in my own cabin made of gold. Not real gold, but gilt, and sometimes I made six, seven hundred dollars a week in that bed, just working the winners."

She paused, thinking. "Men are funny—dumb and funny. They thought because they won at cards they should get me. Isn't that funny?"

Dirk shook his head. "No. I understand it." And he did.

"It went on for years," she said, musing, looking now out the door at the river going by. "Just went on and on and never seemed like it would end but it did. It did. There came a day when men started taking the young ones and I got out. It was either get out or be with the buffalo hunters, farmers, or soldiers. So here I am."

Dirk smiled. "That's a big jump. From the riverboats to a mining claim in the Colorado diggings. There must have been something else in there."

She laughed. "Some. I came west on a train, thinking I would settle where people didn't know what I was and be respectable. I had a good stake built over the years but you can't run from being a whore. Besides, I decided it was boring being respectable. So I teamed up with a man I knew from the boats, a piano player named Jake, and we came to Central City a year and a half ago and rafted down to here."

"Rafted?"

She nodded. "Sure. Lots of the miners do it. They just make a raft out of logs and boards and raft down until they see a claim they like. Jake knew a little and I knew a little from listening to miners coming west on the boats and we thought this looked good. . . ."

She trailed off, sighed.

"Where's Jake?"

"Trash came," she said. "Came on a sunny day like this they came. I was down in the hole working and Jake was up fetching something and they just shot him. We had nothing to take—nothing they could find anyways—so they just shot him. I didn't hear it or know about it until I came up to eat something and found Jake dead by the door there. I never saw them. They must have been rafting down or maybe walking the trail. There's a trail that follows the river but it's hard to use and has to be done on foot or just pulling a mule. The sons of bitches shot Jake in the head and left."

Dirk pushed his empty plate away. "It comes like that," he said. "Fast. Sometimes it's over before you know it's happened."

"I buried him up in back of the tailing dump. There's no dirt so I had to use powder and blow a hole for it. By the time I finished I'd used most of a keg and ruined two star drills. He ain't deep but he's, by God, solid. . . ."

When they were finished eating she cut some plug tobacco from a twist she had hanging by the door opening and shredded enough to fill a small pipe that she lit. It took a moment to get going and when it did Dirk thought it smelled almost exactly like dog shit.

But she liked the taste of it and sat in the door opening watching the river go by, sitting quietly, and Dirk fell asleep that way, his stomach full, watching the woman sit in the door smoking her pipe and wondering what she had been like as a whore on the riverboats between New Orleans and St. Louis.

CHAPTER 12

DAYS mixed. Became two weeks, then another. One day it rained, with wild thunder and lightning that seemed to be right around the shack, in his brain. Some cracked so close he could smell the burn of them.

But mostly it was sunny and hotter than he'd ever known during the day, and chilly to the point of needing a fire at night and all the days and nights moved into one so that he didn't really think in terms of time so much as events.

There was the day he first stood and walked.

His legs worked fine—which was something he had worried about. But the skin on his back seemed wrong somehow, like it was healing on a bias, and it stretched funny when he moved.

The charge had apparently raked across his shoulders from left to right, getting deeper as it moved, just missing the spine but getting into the meat of his right shoulder and shredding the skin all along the shot path.

"I got twelve balls," Carmen said when he asked. "There's nine to a shell and if he shot both barrels that's eighteen. Some of them may have skipped out but there could still be six in there."

Indeed, one ball worked out into the bandage on its own.

But there came a day when he just couldn't lie on his face any longer without feeling like a snake.

Carmen was working down in her mine—"in the asshole," as she put it. Dirk was lying on the spare bunk—what had been Jake's bed—and he decided it was enough. He had to walk.

He slid off the bed sideways and propped himself up on his elbows so that he was standing on his knees. Then he grabbed a stud on the wall, got his hand up to a cross member, and pulled himself up with his left hand.

The pain was staggering and he nearly passed out. But he held the wall, held while he wavered, and it passed.

His legs felt like rubber but they held, his body held and he walked—staggered—along the wall to the door opening and went outside, stepping down to the ground as if walking on eggs.

He stood, looking at the river, feeling the sun on his bare back—uncovered since the wound had scabbed over—and breathed deeply, feeling only a twinge of pain when his chest expanded.

It was good to be alive, he thought, then smiled at the silliness of the thought. No, it was great to be alive, it was *everything* to be alive.

One more thing, he thought.

He wasn't working right yet and there was one more thing.

He raised his right arm out to the side. It stopped before it came shoulder high. Just stopped. There was a tightness across the shoulders, inside the right shoulder, some muscle tightness he didn't understand and he pushed against it, raising and forcing the arm until the pain was overwhelming and he nearly dropped.

He lowered the arm then and when the wave had passed he raised it again, then down and up again until he could reach above his head. Not straight up, but higher than the shoulder and when he had that he stopped.

Everything seemed to be working. Legs, arms, back, body. . . .

Luck. Just luck. If the charge had been a little to the side it would have torn his neck in half.

Of course if it had been a little the other way it would have missed altogether.

Luck.

"Well, aren't you the spry one?"

He turned to see Carmen walking out of a hole in the rock face around a boulder next to the cabin. From his prone position Dirk hadn't seen it before but now that he did he saw that it was almost round and that the strata of rock around the opening had been blown so that it appeared puckered around the hole. It did look like an asshole.

"I got sick of lying there—it seemed time to get up and be human again."

"Turn and let me see your back. It might have opened with all the movement." She set her lantern on the ground and a star drill that she'd brought out to sharpen with a file in the daylight.

Dirk turned and she examined the wound. "Nope. Looks good—or as good as it can. I must have got all the shirt out of it or it wouldn't have healed this clean." She laughed. "Hell, I missed my calling. Whore, miner, and now doctor. I could make a good living patching up fools." She turned and picked up the star drill. "You might as well be useful. Come on in and I'll show you how to sharpen a bit. . . ."

"In a minute."

Dirk waited until she was in the cabin and

he went behind a boulder and pissed and never felt so good in his life. To stand, he thought, just to stand and piss.

He went back into the shack smiling.

"It's almost art," she said, handing him the drill and a small file. "See how the four edges go out. When you pound this on rock it just keeps chipping a hole. Pound, turn, pound, turn—that way. Then you put powder in the hole and blow it and get rich. But when they get dull they just sit there and float on the dust. So you sharpen it this way, so the little point is sharp and the edges will peel your fingernail."

She showed him and he sat at the table with the file sharpening the bit while she heated up the stove and bacon and beans. She cooked one pot every four days, which they heated and ate until it was gone.

Then another.

Plus Arbuckle coffee that she mashed in some sacking on a rock with the back of a single-bladed axe.

"Jesus," she said, "I'm sick of beans. I used to eat oysters and steak on the boats, brought to me by liveried servants. And ground goose livers on little pieces of bread and the best champagne. . . ."

Dirk agreed about the beans. It had been two weeks now, hell, three and more, over a month since he left Denver, all on bacon and beans.

But he didn't want to appear ungrateful. Food was food and he'd seen plenty of people starving during the war. It didn't matter what kind of food you ate when you didn't have any.

Besides, there was something else on his mind. The bit was so sharp the edges of the ridges shaved his thumbnail like a razor and he set it aside.

"Did you say it was eleven miles back to Central City?" he asked.

She turned from the stove. "By river or that trail up above—which is just a game trail. About eleven miles. You ain't thinking of walking it, are you?"

"We need supplies and I thought I might ask around. . . ."

"About who shot you, right?" She shook her head. "That's crazy. Whoever did it will know you and you won't know them. You might just as well put your ass back in the meat grinder." She sighed. "Do you remember a thing about that night?"

He shook his head. "Just the ball of flame from the shotgun. Nothing else. But I know some people in Central City and they might be able to help." He was thinking of Ben and Sam and Burdock. Burdock must know everything going on in the town.

Something nudged him then, when he thought of the names, but he couldn't think what and he shrugged. Or at least his left shoulder shrugged. "They might have heard something."

Carmen shook her head. "You ain't well enough for that trail yet. It's not a road, mind—you have to climb in some places."

He felt stubborn. "There's something else. I need a gun. I lost mine when they took me. . . ."

"Hell, is that all? You men and guns. Act like they mean something. I've got a gun you can have."

She had an old single barrel shotgun in the corner she kept "for claim jumpers," and Dirk shook his head.

"I mean a handgun." It felt wrong not to have one. He'd worn a revolver for so long even lying on the bed felt strange without three pounds of steel on his leg. "I need a gun," he repeated.

"I said I've got one." She pushed the bean pot back to a cooler part of the stove and went to a sack hanging on the wall.

"Jake had a Colt that he wore on the boats. It didn't do him a goddamn bit of good when the trash came on him but he was proud of it. It seemed stupid to bury it with him so I saved it."

She dug in the sack and pulled out an object wrapped in greasy rags. She dropped it on the table in front of Dirk.

He unwrapped it and found not just a Colt

but a presentation model. It was nickel-plated and shone silver and had ivory grips, each carved with an eagle with wings extended.

He brought it to half-cock and the cylinder rotated freely. "It's beautiful—how did he get it?" The presentation models were usually only given to royalty or other famous people.

"He won it off some Englishman in a poker game." She smiled. "Jake was sure fond of that gun. I think he favored it over me."

It was a forty-five—a standard thumbuster except that it was gussied up. "Do you have shells for it?"

"In the sack there's a couple of boxes. Plus you had some in your belt, if they're any good." She pointed to the corner by the door where his gun belt hung. He had not thought of it until this moment and he went to it as if to an old friend.

The leather had dried stiff—the belt felt like a board—and he brought it back to the table.

She had put two plates of beans on the table and they ate quickly and after eating he took the bacon grease container and rubbed grease into the leather until the belt and holster were supple and loose. By then it was dark and she lighted the lantern and set it on the table.

With the belt and holster reworked he turned to the gun. She had a small set of tools she used for working with fuses and caps and crimpers when she could get dynamite and she brought them out.

He took the Colt completely apart, every screw out and on the table on a rag. He cleaned each part with lamp oil—there was little rust but some powder residue, and when each item was clean he started to use bacon fat to lubricate them and protect them but hesitated because of the salt in it.

"Have you got any kind of oil or grease?"

She was sitting across the table, leaned back against the wall, watching him and sipping coffee.

"I think so—Jake had something in a bag he brought with him."

She rummaged around in a pile of junk in a corner and came up with a small metal can of sperm oil.

"Perfect," Dirk said. She went back to watching as he coated each piece with oil and wiped them off.

"It's like watching a doctor," she said. "Or no, maybe more like a jeweler. . . ."

He looked up. The Colt was back together and he worked the cylinder around three or four times, listened to it move, felt the trigger let off. "Guns are just tools—they work as good as you let them work."

"You act like that's what you do."

"What?"

"Guns. I never asked you what you do. Are you a robber? Do you do guns?"

He laughed. "Not even close. I guess I'm a bum—just a saddle bum. I was in the war and after that I just started to move and I'm still moving."

"How did you come to the diggings?"

He realized then that she must be burning with curiosity. He'd been with her over a month and every night since he was able they sat and chatted but she had never asked and he'd never told her what had happened, how it happened.

He told her now—all the way from Denver to Holtzer to selling the berries in Central City. Then down the road until the ball of noise and flame took him and he could remember nothing.

"And now you're going to go find them, the men who did this to you?"

He nodded, held up the gun. "When I can move good and handle this. I've got some work to do first. It ain't much."

"I think you're making a mistake."

He said nothing, looked at her.

"Stay here. I need help and I'll make you a full partner. We'll work the vein down until it plays out, then find another hole." She sighed. "I didn't tell you but I've hit it fine here, ninety and fine. I'm into a pure vein you can almost cut out with a knife. I guess you could say I'm rich."

He stared at her. "And you'd do that? Give me half of it and you don't even know me?"

"I know you better than I knew most men. And what's the difference? I'm an old lady, what do I need with money?"

Dirk studied her for a long time in the lamplight, thinking, then shook his head. "I can't. Maybe I could come back, but I've got to take care of this other business first."

"You won't," she said, shaking her head sadly. "You won't come back. Even if you live you won't come back. Don't lie to an old whore. . . ."

And they sat like that for a time, each lost in their own thinking, and let the night take them.

CHAPTER

13

HE needed his body back and he worked at it. The wound had left him torn, but perhaps worse, the lying around for a month letting it heal had left him weak.

He started going down into the mine with Carmen.

He had never worked in a mine before and he found the experience at first frightening and was surprised at the fear.

He was fine walking in, and even when the tunnel dropped to follow the vein—a glistening quartz strata that ran along the right. But when it turned a corner, and then another, and there was no more daylight, it felt like the world was closing on him, as if the tunnel were going to collapse, and he stopped.

They were wearing carbide lamps—Dirk wore Jake's light—so there was light, plenty to see and to work, and she turned to him when he stopped.

"Come on. It's all right. You get used to the closed-in feeling. . . ."

And she was right. In a couple of hours in the first day he was accustomed to the closeness—although it felt wonderful when they came out in the daylight again that first day.

He could not do much at first. She was working the quartz vein, essentially digging just the gold out of it. A bigger operation would have taken all the quartz, crushed it and separated the gold, but she didn't have the machinery.

She used a pick on the vein when she could—and she was correct about almost cutting it out. Sometimes the point of the pick shone golden in the light from cutting into the gold.

And the gold took him. He thought he would not feel the pull. He had felt something when he'd seen the five thousand in gold for Holtzer's strawberries.

But this was different. Here the gold lay in a glistening line, a small river of it, with fingers that reached out into the quartz pulling, calling, dragging him.

She had struck it truly rich. In that first day he helped her extract what he thought must be close to two pounds of pure gold and it had not been a good day because he could not work well.

He held the drill for her while she pounded, turning it a half a turn with each blow but he could not use the hammer. He helped her pack the holes with black powder.

"I'd rather use dynamite," she said. "It's easier and a whole lot safer. But you can't get it and it was easier to bring kegs of powder in."

When they got ready to blow she lighted the fuse with her carbide lamp and they went back around two bends in the tunnel.

"One would be enough," she said. "They're low charges. But two is more comfortable."

The blast was little more than a muffled thump and when they came back to the mine face Dirk was surprised to see the quartz and rock crumbled and lying in a cloud of dust. It didn't seem possible for so much to come from such a small sound.

And there was more gold. The vein widened if anything and Dirk knew he was a fool for leaving it. He could be rich.

But that first day and each day when he finished in the mine he stood on the riverbank with the gun. Always the gun.

He had never been a good shot—always just aimed at the center of the biggest part and tried to get something in it—but at first he wasn't shooting anyway. His whole right side was new to him and he needed to retrain it. The wound had torn muscles and tendons, reshaped his body, and changed the way his right arm and hand worked.

He stood on the riverbank in the late afternoon and evening and worked with the gun.

Just holding it, bringing it up, seeing where it came to in front of him.

He felt like a baby.

A baby with a shiny toy. A pretty silver revolver to play with.

But he worked at it. The first days, especially, it frightened him because when he started he realized how much the wound had damaged him. The gun either came up only halfway or shot up nearly over his head. He couldn't get it to settle on a point in front of him.

He tied a piece of rawhide around his wrist and to his belt and adjusted it to the right length so that when he brought the gun up it would stop at eye level.

Again and again he tried, frustrated. His eye would see and send the message to his arm but without the cord the arm seemed to have a life of its own.

Finally, by the third day, he was gaining some semblance of control. The gun came up true and only took part of a second to control. He tried it without the leather cord and found that if he "thought" low the hand would stop at the right place.

Hour after hour he worked at it. All day in the mine helping Carmen extract what he knew to be a fortune—thousands of dollars' worth of nearly pure gold—and then at night with the gun.

Until dark each night and after dark, standing by the running river, bringing the gun up to aim at moving eddies, swirls, sticks. Anything. He fired one shot early and used the empty cartridge to dry fire, hammering it until the cap was punctured and gone.

Carmen was sick of it.

"Guns," she said. "That's all you are—men. Just guns and guns and guns. Jesus goddamn, I've never seen the like. On the boats every riverboat tinhorn carried a gun and most often all they did was shoot themselves."

They were eating beans—again, or still, as Dirk thought of it. She had found some molasses in the bottom of a can and added it to the beans and bacon which made a new taste and Dirk had a spoon halfway to his mouth when Carmen let go. He decided to say nothing.

"Like as not you'll just get yourself killed." She took a sip of coffee and he could see that her hands were shaking. She was truly angry.

"These men," he said, trying to form it.

"These men who did this to me—that can't just be left. Not if I'm alive."

"Why the hell not? You were in the war. Shit, men were shooting men all over the place. I lost two brothers in that son of a bitch of a war. And I ain't out trying to find who did it so I can kill them."

"This is different."

"No. It's not. Killing is killing and guns are guns."

And they'd dropped it and finished the beans and Dirk knew it changed nothing.

He still had to use the gun, still had to make his body work right again.

And there came a day when he was glad he had done it.

He had been careful of firing because he only had the two boxes of shells. The cartridges in his belt had taken water and been ruined. And two boxes would go fast if he started to fire. But after a time—he no longer counted days but he thought it was after he'd been with Carmen nearly two months—when he thought he was doing all right he took twelve shells and fired them.

The first cylinder load of six was a waste. He shot all over the place. The gun would come up all right, then he'd jerk the trigger and the bullet would pull so far to the right that the target might as well be in another county.

He concentrated on squeezing and it helped and by the tenth round he was hitting. Not on, but close—within a hand's width of center and that would have to do. He could not waste the shells to improve any more and he loaded the Colt and left it hanging on the wall inside the cabin doorway.

The proof that he was all right was not something he planned and not something he wanted to do twice.

He'd been working the face with Carmen. His shoulder and back were almost healed now and he used the hammer while she held the drill. Pound, turn, pound, turn—drilling a one-inch hole in the quartz face—when suddenly her headlamp went out.

"Damn, I forgot to put in more carbide."

The lamps were simple. Bits of carbide mixed with a little water gave off a gas that went up from the belt through a small tube to a reflector pot on the front of the hat. The gas could be ignited and gave off a usable light.

"I'll go get more," she said.

"No. I'll go. I have to go behind a rock anyway. The beans have hit." And Dirk left her at the face and wondered later a hundred times how it had happened that he was the one to go out of the mine. Little things that meant everything, little turns that changed his life, her life. Like being in the saloon and having a man try to kill him for shooting his dog and taking the strawberries—all of it leading to the mine. Then, just because he had to shit, he went up instead of her.

And ran into the jumpers.

In all his time with Carmen at the mine he hadn't seen a living soul. Not another miner, not a dog. Nothing. Two bodies had floated by in the river, facedown, but Carmen had motioned him to let them go.

"We can't bury them in this rock. Be they sick we might catch it and be they robbed there's nothing to see. Let them go."

And that had been it—two bodies. He'd heard blasting a few times. Other mines up and down the river around bends. Dull thumps, almost vibrations in the ground. But he'd seen nothing.

So when he came out of the mine and saw the man standing above the cabin he almost waved and called to him, thinking it was good to see a new face.

But the man was holding a rifle—what looked like a Sharps. And before Dirk could move another man appeared, also holding a rifle—an old Spencer repeater—and Dirk knew they were not there to be friendly or they wouldn't have the rifles out and ready, aimed down at the cabin.

They were either robbers or claim jumpers—the same thing, really. Carmen had mentioned them when talking about Jake and how he had died—called them all trash—but Dirk doubted there were that many of them around. Miners seemed to be a rough lot and gave short justice. Thieves were summarily shot or hung or cut and that was it. Just like in the cow camps. Yet here they were.

There was a small rock outcropping between the mine entrance and the cabin and the two men stood well above the cabin on a ledge so that they couldn't see him or the mine entrance. They must have come along the trail and worked down on them, Dirk thought.

The gun.

He had to get to the gun and it was in the cabin and to get to it he would have to expose himself to their fire. Out, across the small open area and into the cabin—except that the cabin wouldn't provide any protection either. Bullets would go through the frame and plank wall like butter.

He had to cross that and get to the gun and get to cover.

And he had to do it now.

He took a deep breath, let it out, took another—and fate stepped in and gave him a break.

The men decided to move down to the cabin and to make the move they had to drop back and go around the rock ledge. This removed them from sight for a moment and in that moment Dirk jumped.

He ran across the clearing and dived into the cabin, raked the gun off the wall, let the belt fall, and barreled out of the door—all in one motion.

To run into them coming around the back of the ledge.

Dirk hesitated. For a split instant he held back—what if I'm wrong, he thought—and it nearly cost him his life.

The man in front must have heard his footsteps running because the Sharps came up, came up and on Dirk and looked like a railroad tunnel.

The Sharps fired—a boom that deafened Dirk and it produced a cloud of smoke that hid the man with the Sharps and the second one as well.

Dirk felt the huge slug whoosh past the right side of his head but by that time he was firing.

Working the Colt as he had in practice on the river. All the training took over and he worked automatically. Up and in front, to the end of an imaginary tether and the Colt bucked, bucked again and again. Three times into the cloud of smoke. Then a little to the left where he could see the other man trying to get the Spencer to bear on him and he fired three more times, using his left hand now to steady his right, and the man went down.

And it was quiet.

Some movement, a scuffling came from the first one as death jerks took him and his boot heels pushed into the dirt.

Dirk waited, forgetting the Colt was empty, the gun aimed at the moving man in case he needed another shot.

But he didn't. It was done. The man with the Sharps had taken all three in the chest and was already dead or dying.

The other man—he was squat and had a week's beard—had died instantly. The Colt had walked up and the first shot had taken him in the throat, the second in the forehead and drove him over backward, and the third had gone over his head.

Over.

It was over and Dirk lowered the Colt, took a breath—he'd been holding it—and turned to see Carmen standing by the rock near the entrance to the mine.

If he lived forever he would not forget the look on her face.

She was studying him the way she might study a strange animal, her hand next to her cheek, her mouth partially open, her eyes half closed. It wasn't shock so much as speculation, curiosity. He thought how strange he must look. He'd taken his shirt off to work in the mine and he was dirty and sweaty, standing with the gun in his hand, the clouds of smoke from the Sharps and the Colt hanging around him in the still afternoon air, the two bodies down in front of him, blood on the rocks from the bullet strikes. Like something from hell.

"I thought I heard something so I came up. . . ." Her voice was soft but seemed loud in the sudden silence that followed the gunfire. She pushed the hair out of her eyes.

"Jumpers," Dirk said. "They were claim jumpers. I kind of walked out into them when I came for carbide."

She nodded to the bodies on the ground. "They won't be jumping any more claims."

Dirk shook his head. "No. I guess not." He felt strange. Half elated that he was alive and that he had managed to pull it off, and half sad that he had killed two men. Garbage, but two men just the same. He'd had the feeling before. In the war after a fight when there were bodies on the ground and he was glad and mystified they weren't his—the same mix of feelings.

"Should we bury them?" he asked, knowing the answer.

"And waste powder blowing a hole?" She sneered. "Shit—see if there's anything in their pockets and throw them in the river. Let the water carry them away."

Dirk looked in their clothing and found nothing but some coins. He kept the rifles—though the Spencer was little more than junk and he didn't particularly want the Sharps; it was like lugging a small artillery piece around. Then he dragged them into the water and pushed them out into the current.

At first they caught eddies and circled back into the shore and he had to push them out again and again. But at last the bodies caught the main current and he watched them until they were out of sight around the bend.

When he turned back to Carmen he found that she was already gone, back down into the mine to work, and he went back to the shack, reloaded the Colt, and began to hang it again on the wall. As an afterthought he hung the gun belt over his shoulder and brought it with him.

That had been too close. From now on he would have a gun handy.

CHAPTER

THAT night she came to him.

He was asleep, hard asleep. They'd had a long day after the shooting and a large meal of bacon and beans and coffee and he'd fallen into the bunk like a sack of potatoes. The last thing he remembered seeing was Carmen sitting at the table sewing on her jacket where the drill had ripped it. She was looking down and in the soft light from the lantern—almost a candlelight—she looked beautiful. No, he thought, letting the sleep have him. Young women were beautiful. She was handsome—a handsome woman.

And she came to him that night.

He had never thought of her in that way. There had been some curiosity—she had been a prostitute on the riverboats and he naturally wondered. But he had come to her nearly dead and she had saved him and he never really thought of her in terms of bed—though she was far from ugly and he was healthy. Or at least healthy now.

The first he knew she was there was when she slid into bed and put her hand on him.

"Just lay quiet," she said into his ear. "I won't hurt you."

And she was right. She didn't hurt him and when it was done and she hadn't hurt him twice and was trying not to hurt him a third time he shook his head.

"I can't."

"Yes, you can."

And she was right again except that when she was finally finished with him and wanted to talk to him he was nearly dead.

"That was something," she said, lying back on the bed and smoking her pipe. Dirk felt like even his blood was tired, just slipping around inside his body, sort of running downhill when it wanted to.

"I'm glad you liked it." His eyes were closed but he saw her still on the insides of his eyelids, sitting on top of him, her back arched like a great cat in the moonlight.

"Not this stuff," she said, snorting tobacco smoke from her nose. "You're all right but you ain't the best—not by a long shot. I knew a man on the riverboats that would put you to shame. Put anybody to shame, that man. But you were fun and I needed it. You get to where you need it. I meant that business today with those men."

He mumbled something. Sleep was hammering on him and he was losing the battle.

"They had guns ready and you didn't, right?"

"Ummpph. Yes."

"You had to run and get the gun and then take them as they came at you?"

He nodded and she felt his head move.

"And you still dropped them both. That's what I mean. That's something....

"Listen to me. I want to tell you something." She shook his shoulder and made him open his eyes.

"I'm listening."

"You know how much money I've got? In gold?"

"Nope."

She sighed. "Close on two hundred thousand dollars' worth, buried in a sump hole in the mine. Maybe a little more or less, when it's weighed out. And you don't want to be partners?"

"I never said that. I would love to be partners. But I've got this other business to take care of...."

"Like I said before, you're a goddamn fool."

"Probably."

"I need your help." She said it suddenly, so that it caught him off guard.

"Sure. Whatever you need."

"You'd better listen first."

"Like I said, I'm listening." He was wide awake now and thinking she's right this time as well—I'm still a goddamn fool.

"I'm selling the mine."

"What?"

"I said, I'm selling the mine. I'm going to get out of this goddamn dump and back to something fine. I thought I'd go out to San Francisco and live like a queen until I die."

"But it's just starting to pay well."

"You think that because you don't know. The vein was fatter and is starting to thin. It will get thinner and thinner and I want to sell while it's still fat enough to show good for a high price."

He thought about it for a moment. "What do you need me for?"

She laughed. "For your gun—ain't that a stitch?"

"My gun?"

"Well, that and more if you want but you won't want. I need you to help me get the gold to the bank in Central City and get a draft on it. We have to get some mules and come back on the trail and pack the gold out."

Dirk hesitated. "I'm not all that good at guarding. Look what happened to Holtzer."

"I also know what happened here today. It works both ways."

He sighed. "I'll do what I can."

"Good. Now, let's see if you've got another one in you."

And she didn't hurt him again.

They both went to town for the mules.

Dirk wanted to go alone, and leave her, but didn't think that was safe and he didn't think it was safe to let her go alone to town.

"Nobody is going to bother an old lady," she said, snorting pipe smoke. "They won't think I have anything."

"There's some will kill you for your boots knowing they don't fit," Dirk answered.

So they buried or hid everything and anything worth value and walked the trail to town together.

Carmen was antsy the whole time, with all the gold buried in the mine sump, but they couldn't move any faster than the trail allowed.

It was wrong, Dirk decided, to even call it a trail. It was more a game path, as Carmen had mentioned, and not only would it not support a wagon—it would be damn hard work to get mules to stay on it. There were places where the path cut out over the river on a virtual cliff face, the water thundering below them, and there were other places where the climb was so steep, up and away from the river, that they were pulling themselves with their hands.

"Jesus, Carmen," he said, after one particularly hard traverse. "Do you really think we can get a mule over this?"

"I knew a mule skinner once," she said, smiling at him, "who said you could take a mule where a man could walk."

"But we aren't walking—we're crawling."

Because it was such rough going the eleven miles to Central City took them all day and into the dark. But the trail was well lighted. As they drew closer to town there were more mines and miners and the traffic was so thick and everybody carried lanterns or had headlamps on that light seemed to splash all along the trail.

Except for one brush with a drunk—Dirk simply pushed him down—they had no trouble but they arrived in town close to midnight. The saloons—Dirk thought there must be several dozen—and whorehouses were going full swing, and would around the clock to serve the different shifts of men that came off the large corporate mines. But the livery was closed for the night and no amount of pounding on the doors would awaken the man who ran the place.

"We could get a drink," Dirk said, looking at the saloons wistfully. The thought of a beer made his mouth water.

"Not me." Carmen shook her head. "I'm going to sleep around back of this livery and catch him when he wakes up."

And because he didn't feel right about leaving her alone Dirk did the same. They found some dry and clean straw in one corner of the corral in the back where there was a pen full of horses and mules. It took just a moment to make a bed and they huddled together against the barn wall.

Drunks came and went through the night, and other miners looking for a bed but finally, just before dawn, they both went to sleep.

CHAPTER

☆ 15 ☆

"MOVE. I need that straw you're sleeping on to soak up some shit in the barn."

Dirk opened his eyes to see a man with a four-tine strawfork standing over them. His reflexes took over and without thinking he reached for the gun. But during the night he had rolled over and the Colt had fallen out of the holster so he had to fumble around in the straw for it. Some goddamn bodyguard.

"Had I wanted to poke you with this fork I wouldn't have woke you up, would I?"

Dirk was awake by this time, as was Carmen, and he found the Colt and put it in the holster, rubbed his face. He had never been so hungry and would seriously consider killing for a cup of Arbuckles.

"You the livery man?" Carmen asked.

"Philo Harper," the man said. "At your service, madam."

He was a short man, not fat but stocky, tightly built, and was wearing what had once—Dirk thought perhaps ten years before—been a suit. There had been a shirt, though now the celluloid collar was long gone, and it had been white, but now seemed a permanent gray with streaks of horse shit. The coat was the same; permanently coated in horse shit and even the hat, a nondescript piece of soft felt, had a layer of horse shit on it.

The man, Dirk decided, was almost a walking horse turd.

"I need to buy a couple of mules," Carmen said. "Be they not too goddamn expensive."

Philo Harper stuck the fork in the ground and propped one foot on it and spit through the board rails of the corral fence. "I have a span of four mules I am reluctant to break up, madam. The price for each if I *do* have to break the span is a reasonable seven hundred dollars."

Dirk choked. A good mule was thirty to forty dollars in Denver. Seven hundred dollars was insane.

"I have this man with me," Carmen said, pointing a thumb at Dirk, "to shoot robbers.

Take care that you don't fall into that category, Philo."

Philo smiled. "I have been shot before, madam, and take considerable killing. The price is *still* seven hundred a mule if I have to break them apart."

"And if I buy all four of them?"

Philo scratched his beard. "Five hundred a mule. And cheap at the price."

"Can any of them be ridden?"

"Three of them are broke to ride as well as pull, and they can all pack."

"I will take all four," she said, "*if* you include the rental of four pack saddles which I will return in four days."

Philo spit again, narrowly missing Dirk's foot. "Done."

All of this, Dirk thought, without looking at the mules except to see them walking around with the horses in the corral. And since there were ten or twelve mules it could be any four.

A hell of a way to do business.

"We are going to eat," Carmen said. "When we get back I wish two mules to be pack saddled, each carrying an extra pack frame, and two of the riding mules to have riding saddles on them."

"You didn't say anything about riding saddles in the agreement," Philo said.

"It was understood. You'll get them back in four days as well."

Philo spit again, and then nodded. "Done."

Carmen walked away and Dirk followed her as she led him from the livery to the cafe where the plates were nailed to the tables.

Dirk held back. "I don't know that we can eat there. . . ."

"Don't worry. I know Wing. We'll eat in back."

"Do you know everybody?"

She nodded. "Just about."

She made her way through the door and past the line of men already forming for a porridge breakfast into the kitchen where the Chinese cook smiled at her.

"Missee Carmen."

"We need to eat, Wing. Can we eat in the back of the kitchen?"

He nodded. "Always all right."

He brought them plates with potatoes and ham and clean forks—huge, steaming piles of food on each plate—and they ate until Dirk thought he would burst. Wing kept bringing coffee for them and when they were finished Dirk thought he had never eaten so well.

Carmen gave Wing a fifty-dollar gold piece and stood from the small table near the stove. Wing tried to give the money back but Carmen insisted and he at length took it.

"He likes you," Dirk said when they were on the street again. "That Chinaman."

"Mr. Wing is an old friend." She smiled at Dirk. "It might interest you to know that he is a very rich man. He owns hotels in Chicago, San Francisco, and has a large family back in China that he supports."

"And he's here, cooking?"

She shook her head. "He's here making money. It wouldn't surprise me if he owned a few mines as well as that cafe—although I suppose he does better on food than anything else."

Their talking and moving brought them back to the livery and Philo was as good as his word. Two of the mules were saddled and two were carrying double pack frames and Philo had added a small sack of oats.

"For the mules' sake," he said and Dirk realized he truly liked the animals—unlike many men who worked in stock.

Carmen paid for the mules out of a leather sack she had beneath her shirt—paid in fifty-dollar gold pieces—and they mounted to make their way back to the mine.

The mules proved to be more surefooted than Dirk could have believed—probably better than him. They only dismounted three times, where the trail narrowed over steep drops, and Dirk thought they probably could have ridden all the way.

It only took three hours to make it back to the mine and yet somebody had moved in.

There was smoke coming out of the chimney as they brought the mules down to the cabin.

"What the hell?" Carmen started forward but Dirk stopped her.

His hand fell to the gun belt, then worked around until it was close to the Colt.

A man came to the doorway of the shack and stood. He was about thirty, very thin, and holding Carmen's single-barrel shotgun, the barrel aimed at the ground about halfway to Dirk and Carmen.

A boy—not more than ten or eleven—came to the doorway to stand next to him.

"What do you want?" the man asked but there was fear in his eyes, and uncertainty, and Dirk knew it could go either way. He hated seeing the boy and wished he had the Colt out. Out and aimed.

"You're in the wrong place," Dirk said. "This is our claim."

"We thought it was abandoned."

"Bullshit. You're eating my bacon." This from Carmen and Dirk held up his left hand to quiet her. He'd seen a flicker of something in the man's eyes, a giving, an easing, a tiredness.

"Look," Dirk said. "You don't want this and neither do we. Stay, have a meal, and move on. It's the easy way—take it."

And still it could have gone bad. But the boy pulled at the man's shirt.

"Come on, Pa. Do like he says."

And that worked. The barrel went down and the man slumped against the side of the door. "Hell, it wasn't loaded anyway. I'm sorry, mister, but we ain't et in three days and when we come looking for food or a meal and nobody was here and we saw the bacon it was just impossible to leave without eating."

Dirk stepped forward slowly and took the shotgun and broke it open and the man had been telling the truth. It wasn't loaded.

Carmen had now changed completely and she swooped past him and took the boy into the shack. "Growing boy has to eat more than once every three days."

In what seemed like moments, while Dirk picketed the mules and fed them with the man's help, she had beans on as well as bacon and had put the last of the molasses in the beans. Dirk broke coffee beans and she made a pot and they drank coffee while waiting for the beans.

The boy sat and stared at the bean pot on the stove the way he would stare at a toy and Dirk asked how the man came to bring a boy to the diggings.

"His mother died of the fever back in Denver as soon as we got there. We lost land back in

Ohio and had to come west and by the time we got to Denver we had nothing left. I couldn't go back so I had to come here and he had to come with me. . . ."

He went on to tell the story that seemed true of most of the men in the diggings. All the good claims were taken, the only work he could find was in other mines and the wages weren't enough to pay for food for himself, let alone the boy as well.

Stuck, Dirk thought. Just stuck. Like a pig—and no way out.

When the beans were done Carmen put them on the table and the man and boy ate until nothing—not sauce, not juice, not a bean or piece of bacon—was left. Carmen and Dirk each had a small plate—still full from the meal at Wing's—and the man and boy ate everything else. When they were done the boy used his finger to wipe the last of the taste from the pot, then took it to the river to clean it.

"I don't know how to thank you," the man said.

Carmen swore. "You can thank me by taking that boy back east out of this goddamn cesspool."

"I can't get east. Not without money."

Carmen hesitated and for a moment Dirk thought she would give the man some money from the sack still in her shirt. But instead she leaned across the table. "You go to Wing's cafe and tell Wing Carmen asked if he would give you work."

"Isn't that the place owned by the Chinaman?"

Carmen looked at him, her eyes like gun barrels. "Does that bother you?"

The man backed water. "Nope. I was just making sure. I don't care who I work for as long as we can get some food. . . ."

The man and boy left soon after eating—it was still early afternoon—and Dirk stood outside the shack and watched them go, climbing up to the trail, and when they were out of sight he went back into the cabin.

Carmen was putting the pot back on the rack over the stove and she did it with such power she nearly tore the rack off.

"Goddamn idiot," she said. "Bringing a boy here. . . ."

Dirk shrugged. "He has to be somewhere."

She stared at him. "You don't know, do you?"

"What?"

"Anything."

"I don't know what we're talking about, if that's what you mean."

She sighed. "There's men will pay for a boy like that. Not to work him but to use him. Like a woman. And it's worse in the diggings than anywhere. Anybody who would bring a boy here ought to have his ass kicked."

The diggings, Dirk thought, sitting at the table and looking out the window—Jesus. How did I ever get here?

CHAPTER 16

IT took all of the mules to pack the gold. Much of it was almost pure—"Ninety and nine," as Carmen put it. But a lot of it was mixed with quartz and rock, which made it bulky, and when they were finally done and the sump in the mine was empty the mules were nearly staggering with the weight.

Dirk was nervous. He didn't know if Carmen was right about there being better than two hundred thousand dollars in gold—although she seemed to be right about everything else—but there was one hell of a lot of gold, whatever it was worth.

And men would know.

When they came packing out with four mules nearly on the ground they would know, everybody would know, and Dirk was Carmen's only protection.

He still smarted, thinking of Holtzer and how he had failed, and didn't want to fail again.

The night before he recleaned the Colt, checked each cartridge to make sure it had loose powder, then did the same for the shotgun, completely dismantling it and cleaning it and oiling it before putting it back together. Almost as an afterthought he took a hacksaw and cut the barrel off about twenty inches from the breech. He used a rat tail file Carmen had to clean the edges of the cut off so they wouldn't rip the pattern apart and wished all the time he had a double instead of a single.

He checked the shotgun shells again. They were double-ought and he made sure each had a full load of balls and that there wasn't any moisture around or in the base.

"You're careful," she said, watching him.

"Those two men the other day, and this business today with the man and his boy, got inside me. I'm not moving right yet. I should have shot the man today."

"With the boy? You should have shot him?"

He nodded. "I'm glad I didn't and glad it worked out. But when somebody moves that way, and holds a gun half on you, talk usually doesn't work anymore. If you wait, you die—

and I'm sick of getting shot. I was too slow—shouldn't have waited."

He set the shotgun aside on the table and sipped some coffee. "Tomorrow could be rough and we'd better get some rest. . . ."

As it happened the run into town was a cake-walk. There was a close moment when one of the mules lost his footing on a narrow place and nearly dropped into the river. But Dirk threw his weight into the hackamore and dragged-helped the mule regain its footing and they moved on.

They were in town by midday and Carmen tied the mules in front of the bank.

"I'll go in, you wait here."

Dirk nodded and stood between the mules, watching. There were crowds of men on the streets and he idly wondered what had happened to Ben and Sam.

The bank door opened and Carmen stepped out with Burdock.

Burdock saw Dirk and froze. Half a beat, a second, froze and Dirk saw it but thought he might have stumbled. Then he stepped forward. "Mr. Prine."

Dirk nodded.

"We heard you came to misfortune."

"It goes up and down." Dirk shrugged.

"I'm glad you're all right."

Something was wrong and Dirk couldn't see it. Burdock was tight, nervous as a cat, and two men—two of the three Dirk had seen before when he sold the strawberries—had come out of the bank and were standing on the board-walk.

"I want to sell my gold," Carmen said. "Can we get to carrying it inside?"

Burdock smiled, still looking at Dirk. "Of course. Of course. Help carry it into the bank," he said to the two men.

Dirk relaxed, still not certain why there was such tension, and helped to carry the gold and ore inside the bank.

If he thought selling gold would be simple Dirk was mistaken. When the ore was in piles in Burdock's office it had to be assayed and graded—some almost pure, some degraded—and the price for each pile haggled and argued and through it all Dirk stood by the door holding the shotgun with the same uneasy feeling that he couldn't pin down.

She did not get two hundred thousand. But close to it. When it was all said and done Carmen took a certified bank draft for the gold for one hundred and eighty-three thousand dollars.

The amount—even after all the talk—was staggering to Dirk.

And she wasn't done.

"I want to sell the mine," she said to Burdock. "It's not played out yet by a long shot. . . ."

Burdock nodded. "I'll send a man out today and give you a price tonight or tomorrow morning."

"Done," Carmen said and Dirk smiled thinking she sounded a lot like Philo Harper, the livery man.

There was still that to take care of and Dirk followed her out of the bank and helped her lead the mules to the livery.

"I'm done with the mules," she said to Philo. "You can buy them back."

"I have no need of mules," Philo said, spitting. "The market has dropped out of mules."

"Bullshit."

And so they haggled. She finally sold them back to Philo for a hundred and fifty dollars less a mule than she paid—Dirk thought it to be robbery—and got Philo to let her keep the saddles, which they had packed out on the mules with the gold.

"Now I want to buy two horses," she said when the deal was done.

Philo winced. "It is hard to do business with you."

"Bullshit," she said again, and smiled, and Dirk was surprised to see Philo smile back at her. "It's a pleasure and you know it."

"Indeed, madam, it is."

Carmen bought two horses for four hundred

each—again, Dirk thought it to be robbery. One was a small mare, which she took for herself, but the other was a large gray who was set well and had a good, straight back.

"He's yours," she said to Dirk, nodding toward the horse. "Along with the saddle."

"No—I don't need that."

"Yes you do. I hired you to do a job and you did it. You also get paid." She dug inside her shirt and took out twenty fifty-dollar gold pieces. "Here."

Dirk tried to refuse the money but she kept insisting and he finally took it.

It was the most money he'd ever owned at one time in his life and he didn't know for certain what to do with it.

First eat.

He was starved.

Then a beer. No, two beers.

Hell, he deserved a couple of beers. "You want to eat and have a beer?"

Carmen nodded. "Are you buying?"

"Absolutely. I'm rich."

So they ate at Wing's and drank some bucket beer with the Chinese cook and spent the rest of the day that way, avoiding people until they could sleep in the straw in back of the livery again—there were no rooms of any kind anywhere in town—and it was during the night that the answers came to Dirk.

CHAPTER 17

IT wasn't a dream so much as an awakening.

A word.

Burdock.

Just before dawn his eyes came open, snapped open, and he sat up in the straw and thought the one word:

Burdock.

It made no sense at first. The word seemed to be shrouded in mist, a fog of some kind that he couldn't move away, and he wondered why he should be thinking of the banker's name.

He had been nervous when he saw Dirk.

His face had changed color.

He had missed that step.

But it didn't come together in Dirk's

thoughts until he went back over what had happened.

Three men in the dark, shapes, the roll of flame and sound over him, the charge taking his shoulder and back and driving him off the edge into the river, down and into the river.

And Burdock.

There it was again.

The word.

Somebody had said it.

That was it. Somebody had said it and it was tied in with that night, with when he got shot.

Burdock.

One of the men.

One of the men who shot him used Burdock's name—that was it.

And that was enough.

He sat up in the straw, kneeled and buckled his gun on, and shook Carmen. "I know who shot me."

Carmen sat up and rubbed her eyes. "What time is it?"

"I don't know. I don't have a watch."

"What did you say?"

"I said I know who shot me."

"Who?"

"Burdock."

"The banker?"

Dirk nodded. "Well, not him personally. But he ordered it. He's making it both ways. He got the wagon and berries and sold them, then had me shot and took the money back that he'd paid for the wagon and berries."

"How do you know?"

"One of the men who shot me used his name. Said Burdock ordered them to do something. I just remembered it." Dirk stood and eased his back out—sleeping against the wall had kinked it. "I figure he's setting you up the same way."

"What do you mean?"

"You think he was going to let you get back to Denver with that bank draft? All he's got to do is kill you and tear it up and he's got your gold *and* the money."

"How can you be sure of all this?"

"I can't. But it's close enough."

"What are you going to do?"

He looked at her, said nothing, but she read his eyes.

"He has those men. . . ."

Dirk rubbed his bad shoulder, shrugged. "That doesn't change anything."

"But it does. They'll kill you."

Dirk leaned over. His shoulder seemed tight and he stretched his right hand and arm down, stooping with it, and the motion saved his life.

Next to his face the fence rail suddenly exploded and drove splinters into his cheek. At the same time he heard the blast of a shotgun.

He dropped, grabbed Carmen in one arm, the

single-barrel shotgun in the other, and half crawled, half rolled into the livery barn.

Barely light outside, it was still dark in the barn and he pulled her into a stall to the left, put her in the manger.

"Are you hit?" he hissed in her ear.

"No."

"Don't make another sound. Don't move."

He moved away, across the barn into the darkness on the other side. He left the Colt holstered and checked the shotgun—opening it slowly so it wouldn't click and make noise—to make sure it was loaded although he knew it was.

He had left most of the shells in the mule pack but he had three extras in his work-shirt pocket. He took them out now and spaced them between the fingers on his left hand, ready for quick loading.

They would have to come in after him. They would know they missed and have to come in. He could take them then—one, at least. Maybe there was only one of them.

"Son of a *bitch*!"

Dirk heard a thump as someone tripped and the curse to his right, but still outside the barn in front.

"Search all night for the bastard and then miss him."

"Shut the hell up."

Two of them, maybe more. Burdock's men. He didn't know their voices that well but who else would be looking for them? For him? Burdock was probably worried.

"What the hell is going on out here?"

Another voice. This one Dirk recognized. It was Philo Harper, coming out of the room at the end of the livery. Dirk started to warn him but it was too late.

There was another blast and he heard Philo's body slam back against a wall.

Dirk crouched and moved toward the front of the barn along the right wall, the hammer back on the shotgun. In the flash of light from the shot that killed Philo he'd seen the front door and it was open and empty.

His eyes were becoming accustomed to the faint light again after the flash and when he got near the door he stopped and moved to the side again, holding his breath, waiting, waiting. . . .

There.

Movement.

To the left edge of the door, caught in the faint light from the sky he saw movement, a shoulder, a face, some white of teeth.

He aimed slowly, carefully, not at the exposed edges but back half a foot on the wall where the main part of the head would be, and fired.

The charge tore through the wall and took

the man's head with shot and wood and he went down, instantly dead.

As soon as he pulled the trigger he moved, low and as quietly as possible, across the main part of the barn into the mangers on the other side.

Then silence again.

"Jennings?"

Dirk couldn't quite locate the voice and he kept thinking why doesn't somebody come? Jesus, in the middle of town, even this early in the morning there should be somebody. Isn't there any law at all?

"Jennings, are you all right?"

There it was—on the far side of the barn but outside. Dirk had reloaded the shotgun, carefully and quietly. Only two of them then. He couldn't locate or hear another one.

And this one was scared.

It was in his voice.

There were windows on the far wall and the dawn light made them glow slightly. Dirk moved back across the barn, stood near a window, and waited again.

Breathing through his mouth, waiting, silent again, and once more it paid off.

He saw the edge of a hat coming into the opening, then a face, and he fired directly into the middle of the face.

It was swept away and he dropped and started

to reload but there was another flash, a thunder inside the barn, and he felt a burning across his left side and was slammed back and down into the manger.

In back of him.

A third man.

He dragged the Colt—it took years to clear leather. Dragged it out and brought the barrel up and his thumb eared the hammer but he knew he wouldn't make it. There would be a second barrel, another shot. It would come and he would end.

Instead there were two popping sounds. Insane little sounds in the sudden stillness of the barn and the figure in front of him, in the stall, wheeled toward the two shots.

Dirk pulled the trigger, then merely held it back and worked the hammer with his thumb two, three, four times. He knew he was hitting because the man was down but he couldn't stop. Even when the gun was empty he dry fired two or three times until finally it dawned on him what he was doing and he stopped.

The man wasn't moving.

Light was coming fast now and he reloaded the Colt first, jacking the empties out and sliding the new shells in from his belt without looking.

Then the shotgun.

Then around the barn, moving quietly, stopping often—waiting, looking, smelling.

Nothing.

There were three of them.

He went back to the dead man on the floor and recognized him in the new light as Burdock's man and was not surprised.

Then he remembered the two shots, the pops that saved him, and he went to Carmen.

She was standing in the manger and he helped her out.

"You carry a derringer." He made it a statement, not a question.

"You're lucky I do." If the shooting and excitement bothered her she showed no sign of it. "That man was going to kill you."

"Burdock's man," Dirk added. "Burdock's man was going to kill me."

"And now you're going to kill him." This time she didn't ask, but stated it—a fact.

"Yes. I am."

"I wish I had my goddamn gold back." She sighed. "If you kill him this bank draft won't be worth a shit."

C·H·A·P·T·E·R

☆ 18 ☆

THEY started out of the livery and when Dirk came into the light Carmen saw him well for the first time.

"You're hit."

He looked down, genuinely surprised. "I forgot."

It was a grazing wound, across the fleshy part just below his ribs, and she used a piece torn off her shirt to bind it for him.

"I can't understand why nobody has come to see what all the noise is about," Dirk said. "Or the law."

"There is no law. No sheriff. And killing is nobody's business but the people doing it."

He shook his head. "The diggings. . . ."

"The diggings." And it was almost swearing the way she said it, almost a curse.

She was finished. "You'll have to clean it out some later and don't stretch or you'll bleed. . . ."

But he was gone.

There was a living space over the bank and Dirk assumed that was where Burdock lived. He wouldn't let anybody else that close to his money.

It was full light now, and the street already starting to fill with people. Nobody seemed to notice that he had blood on his side, or was walking with a sawed-off shotgun in his hand, or that the livery was full of bodies.

Dirk stopped outside the bank and moved off to the side. Carmen stayed back and out in the street, below the boardwalk.

He tried the front door and found it locked. When he moved around to the side, to check that door, he thought he heard footsteps inside but could not be sure.

He looked at the sun and decided it was probably seven or a little later. Burdock was undoubtedly up—had probably been up all night waiting to hear from his men—and would open the bank soon. Dirk could wait or kick the door and go in. . . .

The decision was taken out of his hands when he looked and saw the teller coming across the street from Wing's cafe. He was holding a mug of coffee in one hand and a key to the front door of the bank in the other.

He stopped dead when he saw Dirk.

Dirk raised the barrel of the shotgun. "Are you part of all this?"

The teller shook his head. It was a cool morning but there was sweat on his forehead. "No. I'm just a clerk."

"Open the door. Then turn around and leave. Come back later—when it's over."

The teller did as he was told, walking off to the side and away from the door. Dirk motioned to Carmen to leave but instead she moved to put a saddled horse between herself and the front of the bank.

Dirk stood near the door for a moment, protected by the mass of the frame between the door and the large front window. He took several breaths, let them out, and opened the door and slipped into the bank.

It was dark and cool inside. Had Dirk thought of being met with fire—as he had—he would have been wrong.

There was nobody in the front of the bank.

He moved to the side of the door, realized it silhouetted him against the front window, and quickly stepped past it to a position along the wall and stood, listening.

A scrape.

It came from Burdock's office.

Dirk moved to the office door, stood to the side with the shotgun ready, and pushed the door open.

"Come in."

Dirk took a quick look, saw that Burdock was seated at his desk with both hands in sight, unarmed. He stepped inside the office, the shotgun aimed at Burdock.

"The gun won't be necessary."

"Yes. It will."

Burdock smiled. "I wondered when you would get here."

Dirk shook his head. "No. You wondered when your men would come and tell you I was dead. . . ."

Burdock shrugged. He didn't deny anything. "Anyway you like it. The point is they didn't come and you did. Which I must admit didn't surprise me after seeing you come in with Carmen the other day. I thought you were already dead and when I saw you alive I realized you were a tougher kill than I thought."

Dirk shook his head. "You've got hard bark on you, by God. You know why I'm here?"

"I can guess."

"To kill you."

Burdock nodded. "And I can't say I blame you. Still, there's room for talk."

Dirk shook his head. "No. You owe me five

thousand dollars that was stolen the first time and Carmen wants her ore back."

"Yes, but. . . ."

"Do it now. Get the money and the ore."

"It's in the vault."

"Open the goddamn thing."

Burdock rose and loosely, almost casually walked out of the office and into the front of the bank.

Why so easy? Dirk followed him. What was going on here? Burdock didn't seem to care.

He went to the vault and spun the dial a couple of times to clear the tumblers, then opened it, working the combination and opening the steel door wide.

Dirk could see the canvas bags of Carmen's gold and ore inside the vault.

"Get the ore out here, then the money."

"Say this," Burdock said, working. "Say I was to give you the ore and the money *and* fifty thousand dollars for your own pocket and you just ride out of town—how does that sound?"

He had all the sacks out of the vault and brought out a canvas bag—the same bag that had held Holtzer's money.

"No."

"Say I was to make it seventy-five thousand and you ride?"

"No."

"Say I was to kill you. . . ."

Something over his shoulder—Dirk saw Burdock look over his shoulder and he started to drop without thinking, drop and turn.

That was it. That was why Burdock was so casual. He had another man in the bank, ready. Jesus Christ, another man. . . .

Everything happened at once. Dirk saw a form to his right rear, hiding in back of the teller's cage, and saw the flash of a handgun, felt the bullet pass his hip, and pulled the trigger on the shotgun all at once, driving the man back into the wall.

At the same time Burdock was leaping across the room to the desk by his office door, jerking the drawer open and pulling out the Colt he kept there.

All at once.

All at the same time.

Dirk dropped the shotgun as soon as it fired, raked his hand for the Colt at his belt, pulled it, and dropped it as well. He grabbed for it on the floor and heard a shot from Burdock that went where his head had been.

He fell on the Colt, rolling, toward the vault and fired as soon as he came upright. Missed.

Smoke now—smoke so thick it filled the room so he couldn't see.

Another shot and he felt a tear down the side of his left arm and he eared the Colt and fired as fast as he could four times from left to right across the smoke.

He held the last shot.

Waited.

Then a thud, a dropping sound, and he saw Burdock fall on the desk and slide onto the floor.

He aimed at Burdock's head, held and squeezed—no more chances. Kill it. Kill it.

And it was done.

Three, four seconds, and it was done.

When Carmen came in he was lying on his side, reloading—jamming cartridges in on top of the cylinder even when it was full, the bullets falling to the floor.

Done.

CHAPTER

19

"YOU can still change your mind."

Carmen stood on the platform, waiting to board the train in Denver. The conductor looked at his watch and then at the sun. Carmen looked stunning—Dirk could still not believe the change that had come with clothes. She wore a low-cut traveling gown in deep satin and a small hat and had done her eyes and every man on the platform, in the station, was staring at her.

Dirk shook his head. "Thank you just the same but I'll pass."

"Are you heading back up to the diggings?"

Dirk hesitated, thinking. After the shooting at the bank the teller had come back and taken over as bank manager without saying more than three words—as if he expected it to happen all the time, which, indeed, he may have. Dirk's wounds had proven to be superficial and he and Carmen had gone back to the livery and rebought the mules from a man who claimed to be Philo's cousin. It didn't matter. Nothing seemed to matter in the diggings. Burdock's death, Philo's murder—it seemed no more than pulling your thumb out of a bucket of water. The bucket and water didn't notice it and the diggings didn't seem to notice it. Everything went on. They packed the gold to Denver and sold it and she made more than she would have made with Burdock and Wing said he would buy her mine. It all worked out.

He shook his head. "No. I've had enough. . . ."

She smiled at him. "There was that girl—what was her name?"

"Sam. Sam and her father Ben."

"You aren't going back up for her?"

Dirk smiled. He had told Carmen some about Sam on the ride down with the mules and gold—just some. She had guessed the rest.

"No. Sam will probably have other . . . projects by now. I think I'll head south, down into Mexico, after I send the gold to Holtzer's family in Switzerland. I've got a friend down there with a ranch, raising some horses. I think I'll see what that's all about."

Carmen shrugged. "Like I said, you're a god-damn fool."

Dirk nodded. "Definitely."

"But I thank you for your help just the same. . . ."

"You paid for it." Dirk had a thousand in gold in his pocket. "No thanks necessary."

"All aboard!" the conductor yelled, though he was not two feet from Carmen's ear and she jumped.

She turned without another word and climbed the steps onto the train and Dirk turned and started to walk away.

There was a rattling as the train jerked the slack out of the cars and started to move and he turned back, tried to see her at the window.

They saw each other at the same time and she raised a hand, a small gesture, then turned to say something to the man sitting next to her and the train was gone.

Dirk looked up at the sun. Midday. If he humped he could get the letter and gold off and buy a horse and get out of town. Get into some country and away from people.

He started to walk faster. It was time to be alone for a while.

Paul Garrisen is the pseudonym of
a full-time writer who lives
with his wife in Minnesota.